SEEING RED

WOLFF BROTHERS
BOOK 1

DARA GIRARD

ILORI
Press Books, LLC

ISBN: 978-1-949764758

SEEING RED

Published by ILORI Press Books

ILORI PRESS BOOKS, LLC

P.O. Box 10332

Silver Spring, MD 20914

www.iloripressbooks.com

BOOKS BY DARA GIRARD

Kayode Sisters

The Language of Flowers

Sooner or Later

Ladies of the Pen

Words of Seduction

Pages of Passion

Beneath the Covers

Duvall Sisters

The Glass Slipper Project

Taming Mariella

A Reluctant Hero

The Black Stockings Society

Power Play

A Gentleman's Offer

Body Chemistry

Round the Clock

Return of the Black Stockings Society

Playing for Keeps

After Hours

A Private Affair

Just One Look

The Daughters of Winston Barnett

Remember My Name

Illusive Flame

Winterwood Lane

1

———

The wind howled.

Damian Wolff resisted the urge to howl back. He would not lose against the sudden onslaught of the wind (its warm breath, making him briefly forget it was late autumn and not early spring) that threatened to rip off the shutter he was determined to hammer in place.

The weather app on his phone said he had another twenty minutes before the rain would start. It was his fault he was in this predicament. He'd been running late to help his father with the house—it was a project he'd put off, until the weather report made it more urgent. He'd planned to secure all the shutters before the storm hit.

He glanced up at the grim sky, the angry gathering of dark clouds covering the tiny remnants of an ocean blue. At first the wind teased the leaves and made them shiver as it danced along the azalea bushes in front of the house, then it became bold and decided to rip a few leaves free, sending them swirling upwards before they fell to the ground. Fortunately, he was almost done on the two story house and the weatherworn maroon shutters.

A triangle of light appeared to his left side. Damian turned and saw his father standing in the door, motioning him towards him. Damian waved him off, motioning him to go back inside, waving his forefinger to let him know he had one more thing left to do, determined to nail the shutter in place.

The triangle of light disappeared along with his father so that Damian could refocus on finishing his project.

A large rain droplet landed on his hand the exact moment he hit the final nail. The clouds above had completely blotted out the remaining blue plunging the fall afternoon into night. The rain scented wind gained speed.

He saw his father peek his head out again, worry etched on his face, and Damian gave him the signal that he was done and let him know he was coming.

He gathered his tools and headed up the porch steps then paused when he noticed one of the boards was lose. He leaned forward to inspect it when something strong and firm wrapped around his forearm. He turned to the bulky, silver haired man with the diamond stud earring who'd grabbed his arm. Although his adopted father was a head shorter than he was, Damian would rather fight a grizzly bear than this man.

"It'll keep," his father shouted, and added something else Damian couldn't hear because the wind carried his words away and the rain drowned them out.

Damian frowned and turned back to the stairs, quickly assessing what needed to be done. Left unattended someone could get hurt. "Just making a mental note because I can—"

His father tugged him closer towards the front door. "You can come back later for that. It's not going anywhere."

With a resigned sigh, Damian allowed the older man to drag him away. A part of him reluctant to go inside, feeling he deserved to be pounded by the wind and soaked by the rain, to combat the ever increasing numbness he was beginning to feel; to tame the restlessness that warred within him.

Damian closed the front door, hung up his coat and took off his boots, briefly squinting against the harsh lights in the foyer that made the entrance feel as welcoming as a hospital ward. His father was using the wrong light bulbs. But that was no surprise to Damian, Eldin Wolff took little interest in such domestic matters. The Caribbean born businessman, with a past as shady as an underpass at midnight, cared about three things: his health, his sons and vinegar on chips, few else mattered, especially in retirement.

Damian made another mental note to replace the bulbs, knowing his father wouldn't care until one of them blew. "If I hadn't been late—"

"I'm glad you came at all." His father turned and headed to the living room. "Why are you determined to do work that I can hire others to do?"

"Because you won't call in help."

"I would if it wasn't the only reason you'd drop by."

It wasn't too far from the truth. Damian wasn't good at sitting and chatting, he didn't feel he made the best company unless he was doing something.

And the search continues for Lauren Metcliff...

Damian glanced at the flat screen TV mounted on the mustard colored wall and saw the face of the missing woman. The daughter of some well-connected New York family that was rich enough to make a black woman's disappearance seem important.

He'd already seen the story on his phone on a number of

his news feeds and social media accounts. He briefly remembered the strangely visceral response he'd had to the image of a brown skinned woman with chocolate colored freckles, her thick dark hair pulled back into two severe braids and brown eyes that haunted him. Although she was smiling in the picture, a photo clearly taken at some fundraiser, which he guessed from the dark blue gown she wore to the large chandelier hanging in the background, her smile seemed strained and didn't reach her eyes. He'd closed the story, feeling a chill race through him, not knowing why her face bothered him. He couldn't understand why he didn't like looking at her photograph and yet also being strangely drawn to look at it again.

He didn't wish her any harm but didn't really care much either. He had other things to think about.

She was last seen leaving a boutique store in the Soho District.

"Your phone's been ringing." His father lifted Damian's cell phone off of the coffee table and handed it to him.

Damian didn't take it. Instead he noticed the coffee table or rather the items on it next to the series of newspapers: *The Wall Street Journal* and *The New York Times* plus a copy of *Caribbean Times* so old and yellowed it looked as if it were from another century (which wouldn't be too far of a stretch), a foot high stack of issues of *The Economist* magazine and big book of crosswords. Damian had given up on getting his seventy-four year old father to read the digital edition of the magazines and newspaper. Only one thing interested him. "Why do you have six remotes?"

"I need them."

She's on a special medication so her life may be in danger. Any information you know could be vital...

Damian walked over to the coffee table and pointed to the wall. "You have one flat screen and no other devices in this room."

"That's where you're wrong." Eldin rocked on his heels with a smug grin. "I've got my DVD player and my VHS and CD player—"

"Wait. Did you just say VHS?"

Eldin briefly looked like a little boy caught stealing cookies. "I got it from a friend. I have a hundred cassettes in the basement." He pointed at him. "Don't look at me that way. There are still a bunch of classics they haven't converted to DVD."

"Like *Rilina the Elephant Queen*?" Damian said with a smile. His father had a soft spot for direct to video, B-movies featuring black actors from the early nineties no one had ever heard of, especially if the movie involved a busty, scantily clad woman doing improbable fight scenes. Some of the covers for the movies were so scintillating that merely staring at the cover had gotten Damian through puberty. But his father found few things inappropriate to show his sons.

When he'd decided to adopt Damian and his two brothers, he'd been a single man in his forties who'd only recently decided to stop sleeping with women married to his business rivals.

"An unacknowledged gem," Eldin said with pride. "That actress was amazing and I have—"

"The entire collection," Damian finished knowing the refrain. "You're right, they're hard to find. But you don't need a separate DVD player. You can play your DVDs on the flat screen. I've shown you the slot on the side, remember? And you can watch other movies through—"

Eldin held up his hands in surrender. "Streaming, I

know. I just recently started using a keyboard and stopped chiseling text into stone."

"Very funny."

"I like modern convenience but I also like having tangible things around me."

"Okay," Damian lifted two more remotes, "this is for the flat screen. And I assume this is for the lovely museum piece over there?" He motioned to the lower section of the entertainment center.

"Yes, my radio."

Damian wisely decided not to argue, instead he waved a small thin remote. "What's this for?"

Eldin shrugged.

Damian blinked surprised. "You don't know?"

He shrugged again.

"Then you don't need it."

"But I *might* need it." Eldin snatched the remote and held it close to his chest like it was a treasured gift. He held out the cell phone. "You worry about your business and I'll worry about mine."

Damian sighed and looked down at his cell phone. "They didn't leave a message." He sighed again when he recognized the number: Sandra's.

2

———————

*S*he'd called three times. For some reason she never left messages. She told him that she didn't want to bother him never understanding that not knowing *why* she called was even more stressful.

He sighed and walked into the kitchen to get away from the TV and the coverage of another bombed city—the devastation making it hard to decipher if it was in the Middle East, Europe or Africa.

"What's up?" Damian said the moment Sandra answered the phone.

"What do you mean?"

Damian leaned against the L-shaped counter. "Why did you call me?"

"I didn't call you."

"You called me three times."

"It must have been a mistake. I—" She paused then softly swore. "Give me a minute." He heard her talk to someone but her voice was too low to make out what she was saying. She returned to the phone with a resigned sigh. "Sorry about

7

that. It was Aidan," she said, referring to her four year old son. "I'd let him play a game on my phone and while I was in the kitchen the little stinker decided to call you instead."

"How's the fever?"

She hesitated.

"Sandra?"

"I-it's coming down."

She was lying. He'd gotten used to people lying to him. And being an expert liar himself he'd become attune to it, taking extra care to notice a change like stuttering over a word, a catch in the voice, a strange pause.

"Really," Sandra added, as if taking his silence for judgment. "We're okay. I'm sorry we troubled you."

"No problem. Can I talk to him?"

"I'd rather you didn't. I don't want to reward bad behavior."

"Fair enough. Tomorrow then, which will be like a hundred years to him."

Sandra laughed. "Yes." Her voice grew sober. "Thanks for checking on us."

"It's what I do."

"Because of your promise to Brendan?"

"I don't make promises."

"Because of your sister?"

He gritted his teeth. She shouldn't have brought that up. He'd shared about his sister with Brendan never expecting he'd share Damian's story with his wife who could innocently spread lemon and salt on an open wound.

But he couldn't blame his friend for confiding in her, he kept no secrets. A quiet, bookish kid who had an annoying habit of reading the instructions of every video game before he could be convinced to play it, Brendan had always been too serious for his own good.

Even on the day of his graduation from the police academy, instead of looking happy, Damian's best friend looked as resolute and grim as a major general ready to go off to war. Sandra had barely managed to get him to smile for a picture.

It had been a balmy day when he looked at Damian and asked him to look after his wife and son. Damian knew the job could be dangerous but his friend's words felt like a forewarning.

Damian assured him and told him not to worry.

When he'd promised his friend Damian had meant every word. He just hadn't expected to step into the role nearly five years later. Never thought his friend would find himself on the wrong side of a domestic call with a butcher knife in his arm. It hit a major artery, slicing through key nerves with a surgical precision that belied the rage and fear of the bloody nosed woman, with one eye swollen shut, who'd only wanted to stop the officer from taking her weeping husband away.

Luck kept Brendan from bleeding to death. Experience kept him from losing his arm, thanks to the quick thinking of his partner who knew what to do, keeping the knife in place and securing it until the ambulance arrived. Brendan was able to reach the hospital still conscious.

But luck and an experienced partner weren't enough to prevent two required surgeries.

An eventual murder suicide ended that tempestuous relationship (an event only first responders knew about since the event wasn't gory or sensational enough for local media interest) leaving three children in the hands of various relatives and his friend still out of commission due to an infection that had developed after the second surgery.

Antibiotics had helped but recovery had been slow and he'd been sent back to the hospital to be under observation for the past two days. In his absence Damian stepped in trying not to notice Sandra's new buying habit that Brendan also noticed but was too tired to do anything about. Every other week she seemed to think Aidan needed a new article of clothing. The child's wardrobe was so expansive that she'd had to fashion a rope to keep the closet door closed and every new item threatened to create an avalanche when one managed to open the door.

He heard Sandra swear then say, "Sorry, I shouldn't have said that."

"It's okay."

"But I have to say it."

He briefly closed his eyes and sighed ready for the mini-lecture.

"You're a good man. You deserve a family. Don't punish yourself because of what happened to your sister."

She was trying to be kind. It was the only reason he managed to bank down the sudden rage he felt. He wouldn't think about the past. He was Damian Wolff now. He had two adopted brothers and a father who loved him. He'd buried who he'd been, the mistakes he'd made. He wasn't punishing himself. Being alone was easier. This was the life he wanted. A carefully crafted one he'd built out of necessity.

He wouldn't fool himself and think he was like other men. He held out no hope that a woman existed who could match his intensity. He didn't care to. He'd learned long ago that he didn't have the temperament to mirror other people's lives. He couldn't reflect the normalcy they expected him to share.

So he swallowed his anger and made a noncommittal sound. It was best to stay silent and let others fill in the rest.

Looking after Sandra and Aidan was a duty he took to heart. Not difficult because Sandra was a competent woman with a close circle of friends.

Sandra wasn't a bother.

Neither was Aidan.

It was the damn fevers. They were unexplainable and frequent and attacking poor Aidan in varying degrees.

If only Aidan's fevers wouldn't keep coming. Over the last three days they kept spiking and then disappearing. The doctors didn't know why and Sandra was beside herself, although she tried to pretend she wasn't worried as she did now.

Damian heard a high pitched whine sweep through the kitchen then felt a slight breeze. He put his hand closer to the windowpane and felt the wind seep through a crack.

Sandra cleared her throat then said, "If you're ready to meet someone—"

His cue to end this call. "What's that, Dad?" he said pretending to respond to something his father had said. "Yeah, I'm coming. Sorry, Sandra, I have to go."

"I'm sure you do," she said with a knowing laugh. "But if you ever—"

"Bye." He disconnected and put his phone away.

The rain was letting up.

Maybe he could cork the windows. He hadn't been able to convince his father to move. Damian had offered to buy him another place, move him into a condo if necessary, but his Dad seemed determined to stay in the three bedroom house.

Damian opened the fridge to get something to drink and paused at the sight of how bright and sparse the fridge was.

"Dad! When's the last time you went grocery shopping?"

"Huh?"

Damian sighed. His father had keen hearing and only pretended not to when he didn't want to move from where he was. Damian closed the fridge and returned to the living room and saw Eldin replacing the batteries in one of the remotes.

"When's the last time you bought groceries?" he asked him.

His father didn't look up but a sly grin touched his lips. "Rarely need to."

"This storm won't last much longer. Let me order you something for dinner."

Eldin replaced the cover for the remote and set it down. "No, need. I've got dinner plans."

Damian could tell by the look on his father's face that he was looking forward to more than just dinner. It would surprise no one that his father had a better social life than he did.

"I hope you're playing it safe," Damian said.

Eldin grinned. "Always." He frowned when Damian's phone alerted him to a text. "You've got too many people you're trying to look after," he said, watching Damian check his phone.

"It's okay," Damian assured him, "I like to keep busy."

"Have you eaten anything?"

"Want me to crash your dinner date?"

"No, but I could whip you up some fried plantain and eggs—"

"I'm fine," Damian said with affection. "Don't worry about it."

"But you didn't answer my question. Have you eaten anything?"

He honestly couldn't remember and didn't really care. "Yeah, sure." His father looked ready to argue, which meant he hadn't lied well. He thought of coming up with a better one when he received another text.

Resigned, he read the first one. *Have you heard from Evelyn?*

Then the second.

I'm worried.

The first text he could easily dismiss. But the second text reminded him of why he'd been late to help his father in the first place.

3

The wind had stopped. So had the rain.

The clouds lazily sauntered past the sun covering the long stretch of highway in an alternating display of light and shadow as Damian made his way to his destination. He'd been on the road nearly an hour, the Maryland suburbs long ago giving way to a vibrant array of trees brilliant in their autumn colors—like a fruit basket filled with lemons, oranges, red apples—mocking the proud evergreens on either side of him.

He turned off the main stretch to a two lane road. Then turned onto another path that was more mud than gravel. He parked. It wouldn't be wise to take his Jeep farther into the forest. Besides, it wouldn't take more than a few yards to reach the cabin, which couldn't be easily seen from the road.

Plus he was worried. Walking a few yards could help him think. He didn't usually worry. It was unusual for him to feel a sense of unease that crawled over his skin and made him feel restless. But as dead leaves crunched under his black boots he felt worried. The storm hadn't reached here.

Not that the canopy of trees overhead would have allowed much rain nor did it allow the early afternoon sunlight to get through, splashes of dark shadows lined the path.

As his footsteps grew closer to the small wooden cabin deep in the woods, isolated from the main road and the town miles away, the worry increased.

But he hadn't let Shapiro know that. He'd sent back a quick reply that he had heard from her, which wasn't a complete lie. He *had* heard from Evelyn just not recently, and she'd told him not to worry. It was better not to alarm anyone until he figured out what was going on.

The cabin, one he'd been to on several occasions, felt different. It didn't look different. On the contrary. It looked quaint and rustic and unassuming. As welcoming as the gingerbread house from one of his favorite stories. He could imagine the shrubbery made of icing and windows made of transparent sugar adorned with gumdrops. As a child he had reread the story of "Hansel and Gretel" numerous times allowing himself to remember when his sister was with him, imaging that they'd defeated the murderous witch together and returned home.

This wooden cabin, although it had been carefully crafted by its owner to be as sweet and inviting as possible, housed a woman who was anything but. She was as sly as a fox. The tall pines that surrounded the cabin loomed like sentinels and the cobbled path bracketed by small shrubs hadn't changed.

But the vines bothered him.

Evelyn didn't usually let vines grow. They would choke the shrubs, do damage to the side of the cabin.

Yes, that worried him too. It took a while for vines to grow, how long had they been like this?

She usually came here in late spring and stayed until early winter.

But the cabin felt like it had been abandoned. The two windows facing him stared back, dark and sightless. Usually at this time of day he'd see a beam of light.

He knocked on the door.

Waited.

Knocked again. Said her name.

The forest seemed to swallow the sound of both.

He heard something small scurry behind him, saw a flash of red as a cardinal launched itself into flight off of the branch of a pine tree, sending needles floating down.

He walked around the parameter of the cabin.

He looked through the two windows.

Everything was in order. That was a relief. He'd half expected a mess: Turned over tables, broken pictures. But it was just as he remembered. Except...

Except the armchair was in the wrong place.

Evelyn always had the chair facing the fireplace, but there it was with its back turned to it.

What did that mean?

Damian took out the spare key Evelyn had given him and let himself in. He said her name again knowing there'd be no reply— but hoping he'd be wrong.

The smell inside the house was different too. She hadn't been here in a while. He wasn't sure how he knew that but it was a sense and he trusted his senses.

What could have happened? She was usually very careful and if she had been in any trouble, she knew how to reach him. But she hadn't.

She hadn't reached out to him or anyone.

She hadn't returned any of his calls, responded to any

messages for over a week. Others would think he was being paranoid. But she was too regular in her habits for him to ignore it.

"What's a week?" his younger brother, Lucas, chided him one rainy day when he'd treated Damian to lunch. Damian had reluctantly agreed to go to the fast casual restaurant with him, although he didn't want to. Lucas liked to do what he jokingly called a 'wellness check' to make sure Damian was alright. Damian only agreed so that his brother wouldn't grow suspicious and start worrying about what Damian really did for a living (instead of the story they'd all made up to tell strangers and friends). He didn't want to be a burden to anyone. "She probably forgot. She's getting up in years you know." He smiled, meant it as a joke.

Damian didn't take it as one. Evelyn was too special to him to joke about and any mention about her advanced years put him on the defensive. To him her age was an attribute, not a defect, and she had many more years left. She was sharper than most people he knew. She wasn't some dotty old woman and he'd spent last night trying to think about what might have happened. Trying to tell himself it was nothing. Until Shapiro's text.

I'm worried.

He'd find out what had happened to her.

Fortunately, the cabin wasn't large. In one quick sweep he could see the living room, the kitchen, and dining area all distinguished by the arrangement of the country cozy furniture.

She might have disappeared on purpose. He wasn't sure which he wanted more—that she was missing or had left without saying goodbye.

He couldn't bear the thought that the person who meant

so much to him had left without a word. But it wouldn't be the first time and he doubted it would be the last.

But something inside him said she wouldn't do that to him. She, more than anyone else, knew how much that would hurt him.

"If anything happens to me," she'd casually said to him one hot summer day after they'd finished a mission together. "Take charge."

He drove her home, both of them high on the success of a job well done and shook his head. "Nothing's going to happen."

She patted her stylish grey afro. "I won't live forever."

"You'll live at least a few more decades."

Evelyn laughed. "How old do you think I am?"

"Old enough." Damian didn't know her age. She had one of those attractive older faces that could be as changeable as an actress' with an accent he could never quite place. Her brown skin seeming to be as malleable as wet clay: At times she looked late sixties others, when worried, closer to eighty. But a powerful eighty that stared at life and death square on —embracing one while challenging the other.

He decided to go with the assumption she was still alive. Second, that she wanted to be found because if she didn't she wouldn't have left him a clue—the turned chair—to tell him so.

He walked down the short hall to the back of the cabin and then into her bedroom.

Orderly. Nothing out of place. The chair had been a message he'd figure it out later.

He walked over to her dresser drawer and picked up a silver ring he'd never seen before. It looked too small to be Evelyn's. He lifted it up to study it closer, but it slipped through his fingers. It dropped to the ground and rolled under the bed.

He swore and crawled underneath the bed, the ring seeming to glisten with a teasing glow just out of reach. He briefly considered leaving it there and getting it later, then thought of lifting the bed up but took a deep breath and reached a little further...

just...a...little further...

until, at last, he gripped the ring in his fist.

Relieved, he shimmed out from under the bed and stood, facing the far wall.

That's when he heard the sound behind him.

A sound he'd heard before.

The ominous click of a gun.

4

———————

He couldn't be sure the type. All Damian knew was that he was in the direct sight of a muzzle that could make a bad day worse.

He didn't move.

He knew even raising his hands could be a mistake. He was a big man and brown as an oak tree. Just his existence could inspire terror. He used it to his advantage when he needed to, but now inspiring fear wouldn't get him out alive and find out what had happened to Evelyn. So he stayed still and glanced at the reflection in the mirror. He guessed it was a shotgun.

He should have turned on the lights, although the afternoon sun had been sufficient before, extra light may have helped him to be certain what kind of long barrel it was.

It could be a deer gun, it was late November and hunting season after all. But no, it was clearly a shotgun aimed at him, held by a wisp of a woman wearing dark jeans, boots and a fiery red jacket with a hood over her head.

He might not be able to move but he could listen.

He listened to her breathing, attuned to the note of anxiety and fear. He listened to the sound of how she held the gun, it didn't shake, she'd used it before. She was used to firearms. That was a relief. If she decided to kill him it would be quick and precise not sloppy and reckless.

He waited for her to speak. But she was probably assessing the situation. She had the upper hand, but he wasn't in the mood to be patient.

"Can I turn around?" he finally asked when she continued to remain silent.

"Very slowly."

He swallowed. That voice. It was low, husky and as alluring as a lover's scent on an unmade bed. Not what he'd expected at all.

"Not that slowly," she said and Damian realized he hadn't moved. It was like her voice had put him under a spell that had briefly rendered him motionless. Then he felt all of his senses come alive as he glanced again at the gun in the mirror aimed at him. He sighed and carefully turned towards her.

She didn't say anything.

He kept his gaze lowered. Best their eyes didn't meet. He didn't want to appear like the enemy He had to seem as harmless as possible. Agreeable.

Not a strong suit of his. Especially when he was in a hurry to find answers.

She remained silent and it was starting to get to him. He'd never met a woman so silent before. Usually women would bombard him with questions. What are you doing here? Where have you been? What do you do all night? Why didn't you return my calls?

But this aggravating female just kept a shotgun aimed at him and didn't say a word.

"Isn't there something you want to ask me?" he finally said.

"Why are your hands so big?"

Her odd question so shocked him, Damian forgot his vow to keep his gaze lowered and looked at her.

Their eyes locked. Hers as dark brown as his, but that's where the similarities ended. Hers were filled with terror. Sheer terror.

And Damian wondered if he moved even a fraction to the right if he would avoid the shotgun blast. But as he thought of a solution his body wouldn't move because she held him immobile as if she controlled him with some powerful invisible force. That had never happened before.

He couldn't stop staring into eyes that promised a beautiful, tantalizing mystery. Who was she? His gazed dipped to her mouth—white teeth bit into the soft flesh of her full lower lip.

She lowered the shotgun and swore.

Damian still held his breath as his mind began to spin. Instead of feeling relieved he felt anxious. This wasn't supposed to be happening. What exactly *was* happening? Why did she look devastated?

He cleared his throat. "I'm going to reach into my jacket—"

"No."

"To show you my ID."

"I don't need it. What's your name?"

"My ID—"

"Just tell me your name."

"Damian Wolff. I—"

She turned. "Follow me."

He hesitated. She was actually turning her back on him? She trusted him that much? One moment she'd looked at him as if he were a serial killer and now she was treating him like a guest? It didn't make sense. He felt his temper rising. He didn't like illogical behavior. She was another damn puzzle. A puzzle he didn't need. Was she a part of Evelyn's disappearance? Another clue? Damn, he hated puzzles.

He absently shoved the ring in his pocket and rushed after her. "Wait, I think—"

She walked towards the large picnic basket sitting on the dining table. "I'll make you something while you explain what's going on."

"Who are you?"

She pushed back her hood and threw a sly grin over her shoulder. "Rosaline."

A sub sandwich as big as a football mocked him—he could smell the seasoned grilled chicken, settled on melted Swiss cheese, sautéed mushrooms with a burst of red peppers.

His mouth watered but he didn't move to touch it. He needed more answers before he could trust her.

She didn't ask him why he wasn't eating, which was strangely comforting.

"It tastes better warm, but cold is fine too," Rosaline said then she smiled and he briefly saw Evelyn's smile and something inside him broke. He trusted her. Without a word, just a feeling. He lifted the sub sandwich and devoured it, satiating an almost ravenous hunger.

He hadn't realized how truly hungry he was until he'd eaten two sandwiches by the time she'd finished half of one.

He couldn't remember the last time he'd had a full meal.

Rosaline watched him as she sat across from him at the circular table. Cautious eyes.

Damian, in turn, studied her by pretending not to. With her hood removed he saw she kept her shoulder length black hair in cornrows that gathered at the nape of her neck (where he noticed a faint scar), wore tiny hoop earrings, looked around mid-to late twenties, skin like the sweetest blackberries, and full lips. A bulky sweater didn't tell him much about her figure, but she moved like a woman used to action. He could picture her wielding a knife to harmlessly cut a sandwich and just as casually slice a man's throat.

But her eyes disturbed him the most. In the still, dimly lit room they seemed to enchant him more and more.

She finished her sandwich, wiped her mouth with the cloth napkin she'd packed. Didn't ask questions. It made the place feel intimate. Next, she gave him some macaroni salad, he felt like her basket had magic, surprised it could hold so much food.

Why wouldn't she ask questions? Damn, he was used to that. More like evading them. But he couldn't evade this time.

It was like he was giving answers to questions he didn't want to. This woman had too keen a gaze. She reminded him of his brother Ian who probably said no more than a dozen words a week.

But her silence was different.

The look of terror had gone, a touch of caution replaced it followed by an intense curiosity.

Damian lowered his gaze to the table and froze. A tart

stared back at him. He sat back surprised. He hadn't noticed it before, as if it had magically materialized from her basket of secrets.

Witchcraft the wind seemed to whisper as it pressed against the glass. He wondered why he wasn't more afraid.

Kiwi fruit and strawberries sat nestled in a creamy custard, the crust drizzled with chocolate.

It looked delicious but he was not going to ask if she'd made it herself. He needed to end this meal so he could get back to his search. He folded up his napkin ready to stand, but her low husky voice stopped him.

"Damian Wolff you said?"

He nodded. He didn't want to speak; he wanted to keep her talking.

"Would you like some sorrel juice to go with—"

Yes. "No." He pounded the table. "Are you for real?"

"It's okay. Sorrell juice is out. I also have pineapple and—"

He closed his eyes. If he didn't look at her perhaps things would start making sense.

"Don't be upset."

He opened his eyes and saw she looked worried.

"Ask me a question that makes sense," he said in a rough voice.

He hadn't meant to lose his cool and he certainly didn't mean to frighten her, but everything about this moment was wrong. The attractive dessert, the attractive woman. He was surrounded by temptations he hadn't had to deal with in a while. He'd never felt like this before. And this strange woman made him feel a lot more than he was ready to admit.

A flash of regret crossed her features and he immediately

felt guilty. "I'm sorry," she said softly. "Sometimes I forget people need to tell me things."

He blinked. If that was supposed to make sense she was sorely mistaken. He sighed. "Can I ask you some questions?"

Her face brightened and to his surprise she looked relieved. He wouldn't read too much into what he was seeing, although it ignited a hunger in him he wanted to ignore. "Yes, please."

"What are you doing here?"

"I came to see my grandmother."

His brows shot up. "Grandmother?"

"Yes."

He never realized Evelyn had a family. She was such a solitary, guarded person he never suspected she had anyone else. Now he understood why something felt familiar about Rosaline. She had Evelyn's smile and firm chin.

"Have you heard from her?" he asked her.

"Not recently, that's why I came by."

"When was the last time?" *Please say yesterday.*

Rosaline tapped her chin. "I think it was about a week ago."

Shit.

"We usually talk every week and then I didn't hear from her and I started to worry."

Me too.

"She's like clockwork."

Exactly.

"And if she were in trouble she isn't one to stay quiet so I felt something was wrong."

On target. She had described Evelyn to a T but that didn't help him.

"I packed a basket full of food anyway, just in case she was sick in bed and hadn't made it to the grocery store."

"Hmm."

"But then you were here and you looked so hungry I thought you could use the food instead."

"I'm sorry—"

"Don't be. You'll need all the strength you need to find her."

He tensed. "You think she's missing?"

"Don't you?"

Rosaline didn't look worried, but rather resigned. She didn't mention cops. Strange.

"What do you know about her?" he asked.

Rosaline shook her head. "Questions like that won't help you find her."

"How do you know I'll find her?"

She shrugged. "I just do. What else do you need to ask me?" She cut a slice of the tart and placed it in front of him. When he didn't touch it she said, "Aren't you still hungry?"

Ravenous. Ravenous for answers. Ravenous for the sweet promise of the dessert, but more importantly, ravenous for a woman with a voice that reminded him of a mist filled cave with eyes that settled on him without fear.

Was he still hungry? Absolutely. He wondered if she was testing him. The air seemed to crackle with an unnerving awareness. What game was she playing? He'd never felt this attracted to a person before.

She stood and turned.

She shouldn't have turned and left herself vulnerable. Damian saw her long neck, exposed. Twice she'd made herself vulnerable to him. And that intoxicating vulnerability, the scent of it, plus this unnamed hunger, caused him to leap to his feet.

He grabbed her arm and spun her around. This time he didn't care about the fear in her eyes, he wanted her to fear him. To feel something. To realize that as Evelyn's granddaughter she could be in danger too.

"Don't turn your back on a stranger," he said.

She blinked without fear, instead she smiled. "You're not a stranger."

5

He released her like a man who'd been shot—a quick, jerky motion that surprised them both.

His response told Rosaline a lot.

He thought she was loopy. Rosaline couldn't blame him. She was always saying the wrong things. But even when she said the right things they sounded wrong. Because she was different. She considered telling him the truth. That she could read his aura; that she'd even seen him in a dream once.

No, a nightmare really. He was covered in blood. Her blood as he cradled her close and told her—no commanded her—not to die. And she remembered thinking that no one had held her so tenderly before and then she woke up.

He posed no danger. Except that she'd never imagined he could be real. Never imagined that her life would be tied to his.

When she'd first heard him in the cabin she didn't know what to think. Few people knew about her grandmother's cabin in the woods. He hadn't appeared to have broken in. And why was a big man checking under the bed...?

She wanted answers. She'd planned to get them, that was until he turned.

And she saw her future children in his eyes.

She'd never had such a flash of awareness before. She'd expected surprise, anger, distrust in his dark gaze but instead, so briefly she still wasn't sure if she hadn't imagined it, he looked lost and sad. And for a moment she wanted to rush into his arms and ease his sadness but just as much she also wanted to run away.

It was that passing expression that gave her pause to look past his aura to the man standing in front of her. He had a good looking, life worn face, although she wouldn't put him much past thirty, maybe mid, short black hair and trim beard, but he had extraordinarily beautiful, big brown eyes framed by dark lashes. He was built like a mountain with hands that could crush boulders, but he didn't move like a big man, every movement was calculated, understated, as if he knew how his presence affected others.

His boots were worn, but expensive, but the same couldn't be said for his brown sports jacket and jeans, which looked like he'd picked them up at a yard sale just because they'd happened to fit.

Rosaline had seized on his hands and had asked him the inane question about them because she couldn't accept that her flash of insight was real nor could she ask if he was wearing eyeliner to make his lashes appear so dark (his gorgeous eyes really didn't seem to match the rest of him). How could her fate be tied to a man like this? No way could a man like this be her future lover. He was all wrong.

She hadn't had much use for men, few interested her but

if she had to choose one, he would have been more refined, not so forceful looking, not so jaded with an air of isolation— one he fiercely guarded. Getting close to him would be a challenge.

Not that she wanted to. She was not experienced and doubted she could hold the interest of a man like him for long. She couldn't imagine being held in this man's arms as a lover.

She'd been briefly terrified of him because he represented the loss of her freedom. It felt too soon to meet him. She wasn't ready to meet anyone yet. She wasn't ready for whatever fate had in store. How could fate tie her with someone she didn't know, let alone love? But she accepted it with a feeling of defeat. Perhaps they'd meet again years from now. All she knew now was that he would be the key to finding her grandmother. She'd figure out the rest later. But first she had to regain his trust, pierce through his wary gaze.

He had the beautiful aura of a defender. A caretaker.

"Have we met before?" he said.

"No."

"Then how do you know me?" He paused. "Did Evelyn tell you...about me?"

"No."

A slight narrowing of his eyes, a touch of a frown. Except for the brief outburst before about the sorrel juice he kept tight control on his feelings, but Rosaline could still read him. He wanted answers. She wished she could give them.

Damian glanced towards the window. She guessed he was trying his best not to intimidate her. He was careful to keep his hands at his side rather than resting them on his hips or folding his arms, which would only make him appear bigger. She appreciated the effort. "Do you know where she is?" he asked.

"No."

"Would you tell me if you did?"

She hesitated.

He seized on her hesitation but continued to keep his gaze averted. "What are you hiding from me?"

"I don't want to get in the way."

He paused. "The way of what?"

"You finding her. I know you will."

He took a step back and stared at her stunned.

She gestured to the seat. "You should sit down."

"No."

She chewed the inside of her cheek; she didn't think he'd be accommodating. Too bad.

He rubbed his chin. "Alive or dead?"

"What?"

"Will I find her alive or dead?"

"Alive."

"And you know this because...?"

"Just a feeling. You really should sit down."

He folded his arms no longer trying not to look intimidating. His gaze sharpened with menace. "Tell me what's going on."

"I don't really know."

"But you just said—"

"All I know is that you'll find her."

"You mean you hope I will."

Rosaline shook her head. "No, I know you will."

Damian rubbed his forehead. "You're still not making any sense."

"I know. That's why I try not to say much. I end up confusing people. I'm sorry. Forget I said anything."

His brows shot up. "How can I forget what you just said?"

"We need to find her. Well, really you," Rosaline carefully corrected. "That's why you're here."

"When's the last time you saw her again?"

"Wrong question."

"What?"

"Are you sure you don't want to sit down?"

He slowly blinked, his mouth hard.

"I'll take that as a no."

He rested his hands on his hips. He really did have large hands with long fingers, but they were beautifully made rather than bulky.

"Do you play the piano?" she asked him.

His mouth fell open. "What?"

"Never mind." Rosaline shook her head determined to focus. "You want to know when I last heard from her not when I last saw her," she gently corrected. "Like I said it was about a week ago. She sounded the same as always. And—" She paused. "Did you hear that?"

Damian nodded.

Someone was coming.

Rosaline quickly gathered the items on the table and put them in the basket. "You need to hide."

"Why?"

"Because they sound like hunters."

6

They were hunters all right. They had the right smell. They looked harmless with their deer guns and fluorescent orange vests, but they were after bigger prey.

No reason they should be knocking on her door. No reason she should have opened it for them except that one looked gravely injured, his head hung down like a rag doll, blood soaked through his shirt sleeve and dried on his dangling arm, his other arm looped around his companion's shoulders and even the one holding him looked paler than usual. The blood looked real, the reeking scent of torn flesh also smelled genuine. Rosaline didn't sense a trap.

The man facing her looked terrified. His aura reinforcing her assessment, something else lingered around them, the spectral of death.

They'd been attacked but not by an animal.

It looked like her grandmother's handiwork. When it came to combat, it was best avoided. But if necessary she tried not to kill. Her motto: Wound one, make the other one useful. But why had they come here?

"We need help," the hunter said.

They'd either gotten lucky or knew this cabin was here and had gotten attacked before they reached it.

Rosaline let them inside and set about with her plan.

SHE'D MAKE A VERY convincing poisoner. Damian watched Rosaline from the inside of the kitchen pantry as the two men gratefully sipped the sleep ladened coffee, he'd covertly watched her make, which she'd given them with a gentle smile after she'd attended to the gravely wounded one.

He was fascinated how Rosaline's expression gave nothing away. He should be terrified.

Instead he was aroused. He turned from the scene and closed his eyes. Moments later he heard her footsteps approach and she said, "It's done."

He opened his eyes and crept out of his hiding place. He approached the two men.

"Evelyn's signature," Rosaline said.

Damian sent her a look. So she knew about Evelyn's other life. Interesting. He nodded.

"Wonder why she sent them here."

He wondered that too but didn't have much to say. It was also possible Evelyn wasn't working alone. But he didn't want to think about that. It only raised more questions. Such as why she didn't trust him. She did. He *had* to believe that. She'd wanted him to uncover something.

Just like the moved chair he had to believe these two men were a message. If only he knew what they meant. He bent to search for their identities but paused when Rosaline shook her head. "It's no use. They don't have IDs."

"Both of them?"

"Yes. And I didn't see any transportation so they either walked here."

"Or were dropped off," he finished.

She nodded.

His frustration grew. This was all wrong. He'd come to find Evelyn, but she wasn't there. Instead he was in a room with a disturbing woman (he could have been just as helpless as these two men, he'd eaten whatever she'd handed him, what kind of sorceress was she?) with two strangers with deer guns. No IDs meant they'd been sent on a mission.

Damian searched both men and found they both carried knives, two of varying sizes, a pistol (it was a thing of beauty —easy to conceal with a fast rate of fire), a taser and a pen, which actually turned out to be an ordinary pen to his disappointment.

He wasn't thinking right. Nothing made sense. Rosaline briefly mentioned their boots but Damian hadn't seen anything extraordinary about them.

He felt a cool soft touch on his hand.

He turned sharply to her.

"You're still hungry."

"Will you stop saying that," he ground out between clenched teeth.

"It's true. You can barely think because you've not slept well and those sandwiches and the salad only took a slight edge of a bigger hunger."

"I wish you wouldn't call it that."

"What would you like me to call it?"

He swallowed. This was not the time nor the place. He sat. "Fine, fine. Give me the tart."

To his annoyance she was right. He was still hungry and

the delicious tart helped him to focus again. At least focus on something besides wanting to devour her.

With each bite he thought about his last talk with Evelyn then thought about the chair and where it was facing. Then looked at the men still in the same position when Rosaline'd first welcomed them inside to sit by the fireplace.

The chair faced the wall. A wall cluttered with pictures of places—boats drifting on the Caribbean Sea, seagulls sailing over the White Cliffs of Dover, a lost yellow scarf blowing past a pyramid in Egypt—but no people.

Pictures he'd seen thousands of times.

He stood. Maybe that was it. Pictures he'd seen before and had become blind to. What had he missed?

But nothing seemed unusual. There was a picture of the cabin looking every much like a gingerbread house—this time without the vines.

Rosaline stood beside him. "I wonder what the fake vines are for?"

He spun to her. "Fake?"

"Yes, the vines aren't real."

His heart began to race. That meant he wasn't too late. Time hadn't passed. But it was a good question. Why the vines?

He gestured to the two men. "How long will they be out?"

Rosaline frowned. "Out?"

Damian sighed. "Asleep."

Her frown increased. "They're not asleep."

His voice rose in alarm. "What do you mean they're not asleep?" He rushed over to them and checked for a pulse on the severely injured man. Nothing.

He stared at the second man, who also looked peaceful, afraid to confirm what he already suspected.

38

7

———

Damian turned with the careful precision of a prey animal in the sight of a predator. He kept his voice soft. "Why did you do that?"

"I didn't want them to suffer," Rosaline said so matter-of-factly his hand shook in anger.

"So you killed them?" He didn't give her a chance to respond, rage coursing through his veins. He shoved her against the wall and pressed a knife against her throat, one he always carried with him though he'd been tempted to use one from the hunters. So many missed chances. Why had he so readily trusted her? He felt dizzy again as their eyes met. How could a killer look so frightened? No. No! He wouldn't fall for it this time. "How much time do I have left?"

"Left?"

He gritted his teeth. And that damn habit of hers of repeating what he said was getting to him too. No one was this dense. But he'd indulge her. "How much time before I die?"

"In minutes, months or years?"

"You think this is funny?" He pressed the knife closer to her neck. She didn't even flinch.

"The truth is I don't know when you'll die."

Damn why did she have to look so innocent? "What did you put in the food? And if you start listing ingredients I swear I'll—"

"I don't know what you're talking about."

"The poison."

"There's no poison."

He nodded at the two men. "Then how do you explain them?"

"Oh," Her face lit with relief then understanding. "Oh of course. You poor thing. I wasn't clear. I'm sorry." She cleared her throat as if preparing a practiced speech. "I didn't poison them. They were already dying from a poisoning before. I just drugged them with a powerful sleeping aid. I thought it would be better if they didn't suffer."

"So they *were* poisoned?"

"Yes, but not by me," she stated firmly. "They weren't even aware. Probably thought it was a bee sting or the like. I checked their necks."

"Poisoning isn't Evelyn's style."

"No," Rosaline agreed. "But I still think she's the reason why they're here. This isn't an easy place to stumble up on and I didn't see tire tracks when I looked outside."

"I parked farther down the drive. They could have done the same."

She headed for the door.

"No, don't do that yet," Damian said, reading her intention. She was as curious as he was about the two men but he still wanted to keep her close by. "Let me think for a minute."

Damian walked over to the wall and studied the pictures again. Still nothing stood out. But there was a reason Evelyn had the chair facing it. Why couldn't he see it?

He turned to Rosaline then stopped when he noticed a trickle of blood stain the collar of her shirt. He silently swore. He'd meant to scare her not cut her.

He reached for her and she drew back with a pained expression. "I want to help you," he said losing patience, annoyed that the thought of his touch made her wince when a cold knife blade hadn't.

"I'm not a bad guy." He motioned her forward. "I won't hurt you. Sit down. No, don't shake your head. I mean it."

Rosaline reluctantly sat, bracing herself. She watched Damian retrieve Evelyn's first aid kit then sit down in front of her. She closed her eyes. He was too close.

His knuckle brushed against her neck and instead of feeling uneasy she felt calm. How could her body seem to know his touch when she'd never met him before?

"It may sting a bit," he said, "but I'm not going to hurt you."

"I know." She continued to keep her eyes closed. Almost embarrassed by his attention as he gently cleaned the wound. She was so used to looking after others. It had been so long since anyone had cared for her.

He smoothed on a large band-aid. "I'm sorry."

Rosaline opened her eyes. "For what? Accusing me of poisoning you? Or accusing me of poisoning them? Or for putting a knife to my throat or—"

Damian pressed a finger to her lips. "For everything."

Rosaline didn't reply. She knew that forgiving him wouldn't be enough. There was a dark aura of sadness that swirled around him. He seemed to regret too many things.

She didn't want that.

"Tell me how you met Evelyn," she said.

To her amazement his aura changed with such a radiant and brilliant transformation she nearly gasped. His colors came to life, revealing all the true feelings he had for the woman he was searching for. His expression didn't change, his mouth didn't soften, but his eyes brightened with such a tender warmth she almost envied Evelyn. Envious of being the object of someone's affection like this. He showed a great capacity to love and at that moment Rosaline felt her heart shift towards him.

She dare not call it love, but...

How could she have lived her life without him and now feel as if she'd have no life if he wasn't in it?

"She found me," Damian said, his voice reflecting the tenderness in his gaze, the light trace of an accent adding a musical spice to his words. "I thought people like her only existed in stories. My sister and I weren't living very well at the time and..."

"Go on," she urged when he fell silent, desperate to bask in the beautiful glow that surrounded him. He really cared about Evelyn and loved her with a heartfelt, unapologetic devotion.

The beautiful glow dimmed. Damian stared at her for a moment too long and Rosaline held her breath before he looked away. "I'd rather not talk about it."

"I know, but you need to."

He closed the lid of the first aid kit and stood. "There's nothing more for me to do here. We should leave."

"What about them?" she said, motioning to the two men.

"I'll have someone take care of it—I mean them." He

paused and studied her as if something had suddenly occurred to him. "How did you get here? I didn't hear a car."

"A taxi dropped me off and I walked most of the way. I like the woods." She snapped her fingers. "I almost forgot." She pulled out a box from her basket and handed it to him. "Does this mean anything to you?"

8

———

Damian gazed down at the tiny bracelet inside the box Rosaline had handed to him.

It meant everything to him.

It also signaled Evelyn'd wanted him to trust Rosaline and that she'd possibly left something for him at his place. His time here was done.

He looked again at the chair, the pictures on the wall, the two dead men who looked like they were sleeping, then at the woman standing there. He thought of the fake vines and the unfamiliar ring he'd found on Evelyn's dresser.

He pulled it from his pocket. "Do you know anything about this?"

She gasped in delight and seized it before sliding it on her finger. "I thought I'd lost it. Thank you."

He studied her. "So...you left it here?"

"Obviously."

"When was that?"

She shrugged. "Several weeks I guess."

He wasn't sure if he believed her, but couldn't imagine

why she'd lie. She'd been the one to notice the fake vines. Rosaline was part of the puzzle and he wasn't letting her go until he got more answers. He had to leave but before he did he had to let her know. She needed to realize what Evelyn meant to him.

He looked down at the bracelet made of wooden beads. Beads that represented eight years of life. Eight years of struggle and then renewal. He gripped the bracelet in his hand. The words wanted to come even though his chest felt heavy. Few people knew about his past. He preferred it that way, but somehow he needed her to know the truth. It seemed Evelyn wanted her to.

He motioned to the dining table and they both sat.

"I spent the first seven years of my life on a small island with little prospects. I know it's hard to imagine looking at me now, but I used to be small for my age."

"Go on," Rosaline gently said when he paused.

"You have to understand, at the time I was desperate. I was the eldest and I wanted to help my sister and...I'd resisted for years, but then I had no choice so when this older boy told me there was a way I could make a lot of ready money..." He released a long breath. This was harder than he'd expected. He didn't want to face her judgment but any pity would be just as bad.

"I didn't ask you about Evelyn to make you sad," Rosaline said.

Damian laughed. "That's the strange part. The worst day of my life was also the best day. No, I want to tell you." He shoved the bracelet in his pocket and leaned back. "I got hired out by this guy who knew that people had a...um...preference for young boys. I was so clueless I didn't even know what I was really supposed to do. The guy said do anything they wanted and then he'd give me money. So, one day, I ended up at this apartment. I was so nervous I was sweating. I was about to knock on the door when Evelyn appeared in the hallway and said the strangest thing to me: 'Do you want to fly?'

"I didn't know what to say. It didn't make any sense. But she motioned me towards her and said, 'If you want to fly come with me.'

"I don't know why I did it. I didn't know her, I needed the money, but it was as if my legs moved without me thinking. Before I knew it she was attaching me to her and then we rappelled down the side of the building.

"That night I did fly. I felt the wind, the air. I felt free. I didn't feel scared for the first time in months and once we hit the ground, for a brief second I wanted to do it all again. Then I panicked. I thought of all the trouble I'd get in with the guy once he found out I'd gone missing. Then Evelyn did the most extraordinary thing and said, 'I knew tonight was my lucky night. I'm so glad I met you. You will work for me from now on.'"

"I didn't even think to say no. I didn't even think that she might be dangerous. I agreed. And that was that."

Rosaline cupped her chin in her hand.

"What?"

She shook her head. "That's not the full story."

"It's how I like to remember it."

"Is the truth really so hard to share?"

"Yeah."

"What happened to your sister?"

He stood.

Rosaline wisely let the subject drop. "So you work for Evelyn?"

"Hmm."

"And now you rescue people and that's your calling."

Damian nodded unsure if it was a question or statement.

"Do you—"

"I can't tell you more until I find her."

"But what if your job is the reason why she disappeared?"

"Exactly. The less you know the safer you'll be."

"Perhaps, but it also leaves you in the dark as to what I might know."

"Do you work for her too?"

"In a way."

He sighed. "You're asking me to trust you."

"Is that so hard?"

"Yes, but I'm trying."

"Okay, then I'll work hard to win your trust." She placed a recorder on the table then pressed 'play'. Evelyn's melodious voice seemed to fill up the room.

What do you see?

What do you see?

Do see the fox up in a tree?

How about the beaver down by your knee?

Has the sky turned grey?

Has the sea turned white?

Do you shiver when you hear it?

The lonely ghost at night?

The splash of an anchor,

Tossed from a great height?

What do you see?

What do you see?

Damian froze. "Why did you play that?"

Rosaline turned off the recorder. "Does it make any sense to you?"

"No. You?"

She shook her head.

"When did you get that?"

"A week ago?"

"Is that a question or a statement?"

"I didn't really pay attention."

"Is that what you meant when you said I wasn't a stranger? You knew I'd be here?"

She hesitated then nodded.

Damian stared at Rosaline, slowly coming to a decision.

She knew something but she didn't know it herself. She was the key. That's why the message had been sent to her.

He drummed his fingers on the table.

Vines concealed. What if the strange rhyme gave them a location?

He raced outside with a flashlight and removed the vines near the lower right corner and scanned his beam of light over it.

It illuminated a shape. The shape of an island. He saw a star inside pinpointing a location. *White sea, lonely ghost.* He felt his blood go cold.

"You've found her, haven't you?" Rosaline said behind him.

He turned off his flashlight and let the vines fall covering the image. No, he wasn't going back there. It had to be a mistake.

He needed to get away from here, to his own territory. But one mystery was solved. "No. We should go." He turned and went back inside.

Rosaline watched him, the echo of his blatant lie giving

her goose bumps. She'd watched him closely as he'd listened to the recording and had accurately tied it to a clue. But he still didn't ask the right questions, which meant...

"I guess this is goodbye then," she said.

Damian sent her a sharp look. "I'm not leaving you here."

"But—"

"You're not safe. You're coming with me."

She didn't argue. He may not fully trust her but she trusted him, Damian still found her trust unnerving but also dangerously attractive.

An anchor. Rosaline was his. He had to keep her close. But why had Evelyn sent the message to her? In rhyme? He had to unlock what Rosaline knew. He was confident his place was where they'd be able to think clearly about the clues, perhaps find another one.

At least he felt he could breathe again because he knew one thing for certain. Evelyn wasn't missing. She'd gone into hiding. And she usually only did so for one reason—she'd taken something or *someone* she didn't want others to find.

9

———

*S*he shouldn't be here, a voice whispered.

She's exactly where she belongs, another said.

Damian tried his best to ignore both as he watched Rosaline walk around the living room of his staged apartment. She hadn't taken off her red jacket a fiery contrast to the cool design of greys and blues in the room.

She hadn't said anything in the Jeep or on the elevator ride. She'd barely made a noise when he'd opened the door and welcomed her inside.

Most people only saw this side of him. The side they expected to see. It was best that few people knew that other side. Although he wasn't sure how much longer he could keep his two lives separate.

He'd worked his way up Evelyn's tight-knit underground organization that rescued people—mostly women— from dangerous or cruel situations: domestic, familial or occupational. Across the US (and sometimes abroad) he'd helped domestics locked up in cellars, wealthy wives imprisoned by spouses who made their point at the end of a fist,

50

and daughters facing certain death to preserve family honor.

And with each rescue Damian imagined his sister's face, reminded of the one rescue he hadn't been able to make.

Stop that and focus! He could hear Evelyn say. She always did when he slipped into a melancholy mood. Yes. He had to find out why Evelyn had been forced to go into hiding first. And he wouldn't think of how weary he'd become. He'd learned not to think too far into the future. There were too many variables he couldn't control.

"Do you really live here?" Rosaline said.

Damian turned sharply to her. "Why do you say that?"

She shrugged. "Just a feeling."

"You don't like it?"

"I didn't say that."

"You don't say much."

"And that bothers you." It wasn't a question. She shoved her hands in her jacket pocket. "I'll try harder," she said then fell silent again.

"Would you like something to drink?"

She shook her head.

"I do stay here," he said sounding more defensive than he'd meant to.

She stepped in front of a wooden mask, sent him a sideward glance then stared at the mask again. Her action was as loud as a court accusation: I know you're hiding.

He wouldn't deny it.

Rosaline continued to look around and he carefully watched her. He couldn't help himself. Usually he was looking around at every little change in the environment, but since he'd met her, all he could focus on was her.

That was dangerous. But she could prove useful. That

was the only reason he'd invited her here. Because Evelyn wanted him to.

At least that's what he wanted to convince himself to believe. He wanted to believe that this attraction was just a mixture of adrenaline and worry needing a way to express itself. Nothing more. Once he found Evelyn he wouldn't feel like this again.

Rosaline turned to him. "Okay, I'm done pretending, now let's go to your place."

Damian stumbled over his words. "T-this is my place."

"Your other place."

He froze. How would she know about that?

"You don't live here," she said in a bored, matter-of-fact tone. "And you don't need to pretend with me. Is it in the same building?"

Wordlessly he pointed to the ceiling.

"It's on another floor?"

He nodded.

"Then let's go."

Damian grabbed her arm when she passed him to go to the front door. "What makes you think I don't live here?"

Her eyes captured his, penetrating through all his walls. Fissures of fear and hope coursed through him. She opened her mouth and he realized he didn't want to know why she could tell. He didn't want to know what she saw behind the mask. What rang hollow? What looked fake? He abruptly released her. "Never mind. Doesn't matter."

THEY RODE the elevator to the top floor where there were only three apartments.

The moment Rosaline stepped into his and looked at the row of windows, she nodded as if she approved of the bird's eye view of the residential subdivision spread out below them. The brush of evening settling over the houses in faint orange haze, some already glittering with colorful holiday lights, gave the view an almost sepia hinted nostalgia.

He briefly wondered if she could guess how much he liked to stare out at the view of the carefully crafted homes and lawns, whose charm didn't shift whether covered in snow, sprinkled with fall foliage or brimming with spring blossoms, and pretend that the people inside the various houses were happy.

"This is more like it," Rosaline said, taking off her jacket.

Damian hung it up for her without comment.

She'd didn't say anything about his place. Not that he'd expected her to. He'd gotten used to her silences. Oddly, it didn't bother him. It should. He knew this place looked like a juvenile attempt at home décor. An awkward attempt at creating a feeling of home, but he hadn't wanted to hire anyone. He'd been searching for a feeling when he'd bought the mustard colored sofa that reminded him of his father's living room, the overstuffed loveseat a nod to his brother Lucas' personality, the kitchen held touches of Evelyn's military precision. To an outsider his apartment could look uncomplimentary and ugly but to him it was where he felt most himself.

Rosaline lightly touched a blue mosaic print lampshade and he noticed the shadow of a smile. Damian flexed his hand resisting the urge to ask her what she thought of it. What she thought of anything. He wouldn't show such a naked need for acceptance.

He held his breath when she picked up one of the

romance novels he had stacked, four high, on a side table. It was a romantic fantasy he was halfway through. She didn't open it to where the metal bookmark kept his place.

Her lip didn't curl in derision as she turned the book over and read the description.

But he still didn't trust himself to breathe. She was treading on a space very precious to him. Romance novels had saved him. After a painful childhood, before his adoption, and seeing the worst of humankind (more than he cared to admit) he needed to experience a world where mothers loved their children, beauty could be found in a lover's gaze and love reigned. Through romantic stories he'd learned what a caring, healthy relationship could look like. How people could treat each other. How he'd wanted to be treated if he were in a romantic relationship with anyone. What he could expect. Not that he'd risk it. Fiction was too far removed from fact for him. He was too different. He'd been let down one too many times.

He felt his heartbeat return to normal when Rosaline picked up another book and nodded impressed. She was safe. She wasn't going to make fun. She understood.

He started breathing a little too fast, his pulse picking up speed.

Could this mean...?

Dare he hope...?

Rosaline? This strange woman, who calmly bore the mark of his knife against her neck, who sometimes spoke in riddles, could she be someone he dare let close?

She picked up a third book and gasped. She turned to him and held up the cover of a romantic mystery, her face lit up with delight. "Have you read this one yet?"

He shook his head, still unsure if she would tease him.

"Me neither. It has to be your next one," she said rearranging his stack, "then we can read it at the same time and discuss it later." She looked at him uncertain. "Do you mind?"

He shook his head again.

"Good. Let me know when you start. I admire you. You're so organized, to have your books for the year ready like this."

The year? No way he was telling her four books was his monthly quota.

What do you see? What do you hear?

Evelyn's words flashed through his mind. He remembered the recording again, trying to decipher it. What had he missed? Rosaline hadn't said much. She spoke about the food, the hunters. Didn't she mention something about their boots?

"Why did you mention their boots?" he asked her.

Rosaline thought for a moment then said, "They didn't look like boots hunters would wear."

"What did they look like?"

"Security detail."

Yes, he'd gotten the same feeling. The weapons alone had let him know they weren't hunters, as well as the missing IDs, but he hadn't paid much attention to their attire.

"What else did you notice?"

"An emblem that reminded me of something I'd seen somewhere before."

He went to the drawer and got a notepad and pen. "Could you draw it for me?"

She pulled out her cell phone. "Actually I—"

His cell phone sprung to life surprising them both. He meant to ignore it then changed his mind and checked. He looked at Rosaline with apology. "I have to take this." He answered, but before he could speak, Sandra said in a rush, "I'm outside your building right now and I know I said everything was okay only a few hours ago but I lied and—"

"It's okay. Come up."

Sandra paused. "You mean down, right?"

Damian silently swore. Of course he meant down, that's where his other apartment was. He'd never let her see this place before. He glanced at the time. If he left now, he could reach his other apartment and meet her there and—

Rosaline leaned close and whispered, "Give her the apartment number," and before he knew what he was doing he'd given Sandra the correct number, giving a noncommittal sound when she'd asked if he'd moved. He stood back when he opened the door to her, feeling as awkward as if he'd stripped naked in front of her.

Fortunately, she didn't pay much attention to her unfamiliar surroundings as she rushed in holding Aidan. She looked near tears, her light brown skin flushed, her permed dark brown hair was pulled back into a crooked ponytail. "I'm so sorry to bother you but I don't know what to do. I've called the pediatrician and she said that it was nothing. But his fever hasn't gone down. It isn't very high but it keeps coming and going. He seemed fine, then I got him ready for bed and put him in his new pajamas and he started whimpering and sweating. I don't know if I should go to another emergency room because the one I went to treated me like I was overreacting and—"

"Breathe."

That didn't come from him, but from a voice as soothing as a spring breeze.

Rosaline stepped forward with her hands held out to Aidan. "May I?"

Sandra sent Damian a curious look and he nodded in reassurance. It couldn't hurt. He certainly didn't know what to do and he'd never been able to shock Sandra into silence before. She handed Aidan over to Rosaline and both of them prepared themselves for Aidan to start crying. Instead the child just looked up at the stranger as if as spellbound as the rest of them.

"It's okay," Rosaline said to the child in the same soothing voice. "I know you're not feeling well. Let's see if we can change that."

10

───────

She carried the child over to the couch as if it were the most natural thing in the world.

Sandra sidled over to Damian and they both watched her. She gently stripped the brown, chubby cheeked child out of his clothes until he was only in his underpants.

The two adults continued to watch waiting for a whimper of distress or unease, but the child didn't make a noise. Rosaline didn't speak to the child, but Aidan's brown gaze stayed fixated on her as if she were singing the sweetest lullaby. His face remained enraptured and at ease. Damian had never seen Aidan like that before.

"Who is she?" Sandra asked.

"I'm not sure."

She looked up at him alarmed. "What?"

"She's a friend of a friend." The less he tried to explain the better.

"A doctor?"

They watched Rosaline go to her basket and pull out something.

She set a small, square-shaped white candle on the coffee table and then lit it. It flashed to life with a quick yellowish red blaze then settled into a simple flame. She clapped her hands together before closing her eyes.

Damian shook his head. "No, I don't think so."

"A witch?"

"No."

It took them both a moment to realize that Rosaline had spoken.

"I'm a healer," she said before she took a jar from her basket then began to rub a lotion over Aidan's arm and legs. The faint scent of eucalyptus floated towards them.

Aidan smiled then giggled.

Sandra took a step forward, but Damian took her arm and held her back.

"He can be very ticklish and unruly," Sandra said. "He hardly can keep still during bath time."

"He's not moving now."

"I've never seen him this calm before," she said in awe.

"Then leave her and trust her."

"But why won't she tell us what she's doing?" Sandra said annoyed.

Damian squeezed her arm. "Give her a minute."

But more than a minute passed and Rosaline didn't speak and Aidan continued to smile while she rhythmically spread lotion on his skin.

"What are you doing?" Sandra said impatient.

Rosaline jumped and turned to them with a look of guilt as if she'd forgotten they were in the room. "I'm sorry," she said. "I was just calming him. He seemed agitated."

"Of course he's agitated," Sandra snapped. "He's been running a fever on and off for days."

"Yes—"

"And for nearly ten minutes you've just burned candles and rubbed his skin. How is that supposed to help anything?"

Rosaline stood and returned the lotion to the basket and blew out the candle.

"Are you ignoring me?"

Rosaline looked at Damian. "I'll go to the kitchen and leave you two alone."

Damian frowned. "What?"

Rosaline nodded towards Sandra. "She wants to be comforted."

Rosaline didn't know exactly what she'd said wrong but she saw a flash of anger in Sandra's aura. She'd already sensed jealousy and anxiety and had hoped that by removing herself she'd ease it, but she'd only made things worse.

Sandra took a menacing step forward. "Who do you think you are?"

Rosaline glanced at Damian again expecting him to intervene, but she couldn't catch his eye because he was staring at Sandra as if he'd never seen her before. Since she couldn't depend on him to deescalate the situation, Rosaline returned her gaze to Sandra and did her best to appear neutral and unassuming by offering a casual shrug. The motion seemed to infuriate the woman more.

"I'm sorry I came," Sandra said. "I knew this would be a waste." She rushed over to her son and grabbed his pajama shirt. She started to put it on him, but Rosaline grabbed her wrist with such force she released it.

"No, don't," Rosaline said.

"What?"

"It's the clothes. He can't wear them."

"Don't be ridiculous. You expect me to carry my son around naked?"

"No, but he's having a hard time regulating his temperature—"

Sandra turned her back to Rosaline. "I'm not listening to this." She picked up the shirt.

"Sandra, give her a chance," Damian finally said. "Aidan looks happy now and—"

She picked up the shirt. "No, we're leaving."

Rosaline snatched the shirt from her and threw it across the room. "He cannot wear it. You have to—"

Sandra shoved her back. "I don't have to do anything. Especially listen to you—"

Rosaline took a cautious step forward. "But you will listen to me because you love your son and you hate to see him hurting and every time you put these clothes on him you are torturing him."

"How dare you make this my fault?" Sandra said distressed. "These are expensive and unique pieces from—"

"Doesn't matter."

She patted her chest with the flat of her hand. "Are you telling me *I've* made him suffer?"

"No, that's not it," Rosaline quickly said. "It's the material. It's a particular fiber that's affecting him. I've put some lotion on him to not only cool him but also deal with the affect of his skin coming in contact with the fabric. He's been experiencing a low grade allergic reaction. The good news is that in a few hours he'll be fine."

"And the bad news?"

"You'll have to donate anything with this fiber in it."

"And that's it?"

Rosaline blinked confused. "You want there to be more?"

"What?"

"That's it," Damian said to stop any further misunderstanding.

"I'll do it right away." Sandra glanced at her son with a caring mother's guilt and remorse. She hung her head. "I feel so stupid. Why didn't I put it all together myself?"

"Because it doesn't present itself normally," Rosaline said. "It's not as if there's a rash you can pinpoint. Please don't blame yourself. You did everything right. Seeking help was the best thing for him."

"I'm—I'm sorry about the way I spoke to you."

Rosaline began to shrug again then thought better of it and took the other woman's hands in hers and said, "It's okay," before releasing them. She glanced at Damian then back at Sandra and said, "I'll leave you two alone now." Rosaline motioned Damian forward then whispered in his ear, "Hold her for a couple seconds. She needs it," before she hurried into the kitchen.

"What a strange woman," Sandra said.

Damian turned to her surprised. She didn't look as relieved as she should. Aidan had fallen asleep on the couch. She didn't have to worry about his fevers anymore and yet Sandra still looked anxious. He'd hardly recognized her moments before when she'd met Rosaline's tender care with such anger.

Where had the anger come from?

Hold her for a couple seconds. She needs it. He didn't know why Rosaline thought it was necessary, but he wanted to help her.

He pulled Sandra close and hugged her, felt her body grow limp.

"It's all going to be okay," he said in a soothing tone.

"Thank you," Sandra sniffed. She held him tighter, desperate desire tingeing her words. "Oh, Damian, it's been so long since..." She drew back and looked up at him, but he refused to meet her gaze, alarm bells sounding off in his head. He recognized the scent of loneliness and need. He understood that his friend had unwittingly created a slow-growing chasm in his marriage but Damian didn't plan to fill it. Never going to happen. Not in a thousand lifetimes.

"Most marriages hit rough times," Damian said. "He'll come around. He loves you." And he made a mental note to remind his friend that if he didn't want to lose what was precious to him he shouldn't keep pushing his wife away while he wallowed in self-pity.

Sandra licked her lip. "Sometimes I wonder—"

Damian wouldn't let her finish. He cupped her face in his hands and forced her to look at him. He saw a flicker of unease and felt pleased. "Wonder about anything. Why the sky appears blue or how birds fly in formation, but never that. Ever. Brendan loves you." Her tears dampened his hands but he didn't regret his words. "And you love him." He let his hands fall.

Sandra wiped her eyes and sniffed. "Who is she?"

Damian stepped back, startled by the abrupt change in topic. "What?"

"That woman." She sent him a knowing look. "Doesn't she remind you a little of—"

"I told you she's a friend of...um...a friend."

Sandra lifted a sly brow. "A special friend, huh? You're a dark horse. You didn't move, did you? This has to be her place, right?" She glanced at the side table where his stack of novels sat. "I mean look at all those romance novels. Someone must be lonely," she said with a giggle. "And this place is filled with too much tacky furniture to be yours." She pointed. "That couch alone would give anyone a good laugh."

Damian plastered on a smile, regretting how he'd let himself be exposed—bare and vulnerable—to criticism. He'd made a mistake inviting her here, but it wouldn't happen again. He'd let her believe what she wanted to. He nodded. "Right."

"Actually, I think this place suits him perfectly," Rosaline said, entering the room with one of Damian's sweaters, dark green with two horizontal brown stripes. She held it up and met his gaze as if to say, *I hope you don't mind,* and he nodded in response not only relieved by her entrance but touched by her words. Did she really think the apartment suited him? Did she really understand him that much when so few did?

She smiled and then playfully tossed the sweater at him and he caught it smiling in spite of himself, feeling as if they shared a wonderful secret. And for a moment he felt lighter and freer than he'd ever felt.

Damian handed Sandra the sweater and she began to protest saying she could use a towel, before Rosaline said, "It's too cold to take Aidan out like that and Damian doesn't mind."

Sandra's gaze shifted curiously between the two of them before she said, "Thank you." She held the sweater looking a little embarrassed. "I'm sorry I made fun of your furniture. I didn't mean to upset you."

"It's okay," Rosaline said, "you didn't and it's not mine." When she didn't elaborate further Sandra looked to Damian to explain but he kept his gaze lowered.

"Oh," she said at a loss. She put the sweater on Aidan and wrapped it around him then lifted him up.

"Never mind his clothes," Rosaline said, "we'll take care of them."

"I don't know how to thank you enough."

Rosaline waved goodbye then walked away.

Sandra waited for her to disappear into the kitchen again before she said in a whisper, "Isn't it weird how she keeps going into the kitchen?"

"Hmm."

"Really, Damian. Who is she?"

He opened the front door.

"Is she married?"

He waved. "Bye, Sandra."

She stepped out then turned to him. "You know I'm going to tell Brendan about this."

"Call me when you get home."

"And your brothers—"

He patted Aiden on the head before he closed the door.

11

———

*I*t was over.

He couldn't believe it was over. One less thing to worry about. Something else to take off his plate and he hadn't done it alone.

He hadn't had to do anything at all. Rosaline had lifted the weight off of him, leaving him to feel a little less burdened.

Damian heard footsteps behind him and turned. Rosaline stood with her arms stretched out to her sides.

He frowned. "What are you doing?"

"Aren't you relieved? Don't you want to give me a hug?"

The idea was too tempting to entertain. He was definitely curious what kind of figure she hid under that shapeless sweater. He folded his arms. "I already hugged Sandra."

"That was different."

"I've reached my daily limit for the day."

Rosaline continued to hold her arms out. "No, you haven't." She lowered her voice. "You know you want to."

"I want to do more than hug you," Damian said in a low growl.

"I won't stop you."

He felt suddenly ravenous again, she stood only a few yards away willing, deliciously tempting. He swallowed. "Put your arms down."

"Why do you deny yourself what's right in front of you?"

He didn't know. Didn't know why he resisted the pleasure she offered him, why there was a feeling of guilt, a sense he didn't deserve it. Or a greater sense that it wasn't real. That it would be fleeting. He didn't want to get attached. He didn't want another person he had to worry about. And he'd worry about her.

"I have to think about Evelyn."

"Evelyn is fine. We'll find out why she's hiding. Right now—"

"Right now I'm tired."

"That's why you need a hug."

"I don't need a hug." He turned. "It's getting late."

She jumped in front of him. "Come on."

"Don't push me, Rosaline," he warned her.

She grinned then pushed him, using both her hands.

Damian was so surprised he actually stumbled backwards. She motioned him forward.

He shook his head and moved to the side.

She did the same, blocking him.

"Rosaline."

She blinked.

He glared at her.

She motioned him forward then held her arms out wide.

So dangerously tempting. He bit his lower lip, swallowed, took a deep breath, but he wouldn't surrender. There were so many other things he needed to think about. He didn't need this distraction.

He shoved her aside with more force than he'd meant to. Rosaline stumbled against the wall and hit it with a bang. He looked at her in horror, an apology ready on his lips.

Then he saw her lips curve in a slight smile.

A smile!

She'd stumbled on purpose.

The horror and guilt left replaced by anger.

"Go home," he said.

"But with you I am hom—"

He nearly pounced on her then. The thought so alluring —perfect and yet painful—that it nearly broke him. He wasn't sure if he wanted to cover her mouth with his own or wrap his hands around her neck and choke her. But he knew one thing—he wanted to stop her from saying anymore. He wouldn't let her mock him. She already knew how to hurt him by teasing about something very precious to him—the idea of 'home'.

He held her gaze. "Don't."

"Damian."

"Just...don't." Don't finish that sentence. Please. I'm begging you. Say no more.

But his words and silent plea didn't matter. The damage had already been done. The unfinished word hanging in the air between them even more potent than if it had been said. The word 'home' lingering like a ghost riddled with pain, her words penetrating him like a knife. He could take her teasing but not about that. Never about that. It was as if she knew he sometimes stood at the window and made up stories for the people living in the different houses. As if there wasn't a tender ache that welled up this time of year as he saw families visiting each other, imagining the warmth and laughter that would flow over food ladened dining tables and decorated living rooms. He loved his father and brothers, wishing they all still lived together as they had when he was young. He briefly thought of the family that death had first stolen from him and how fading memories continued to rob from him. "Did Evelyn tell you?"

Rosaline blinked confused. "Tell me what?"

It was worst that she'd pretended not to know. Why would Evelyn think to hurt him this way?

But he swiftly rejected the idea. She wouldn't. Not Evelyn. He trusted her too much and knew she wouldn't casually share his history with someone else. He'd overreacted to Rosaline's simple joke and felt a wave of embarrassment. This was why he couldn't be in a relationship. This was why he was better off alone. Rosaline wasn't an anchor, she was a reminder. A reminder of why things had to remain the way they were.

"Don't say things you don't mean," he said, feeling the weight of his shame.

"But I—"

"Just don't."

She nodded.

He silently swore.

Rosaline confused him. Made him feel too much when he didn't want to feel at all. He glanced at her wicker basket and briefly let himself remember how tender she'd been with Aidan. None of that mattered now. Nothing could fix his foolish behavior. "You said I'd find Evelyn and I will. Take your things and leave," he said in a curt tone, his unease making his words sound harsher than he'd meant them to.

But Rosaline needed to go.

He needed to get far away from her.

But he also had to make sure she stayed safe. He grabbed a sticky note and wrote down Shapiro's number. "Memorize this number and then burn it. Call him and he'll tell you where you can stay until I can figure out what's going on."

He shoved the note in her hand, walked into his bedroom and closed the door.

12

---

e took a deep breath. He needed to focus.

He sat on the side of the bed and gripped his hands together. Control. He had to stay in control. That he'd lost his temper wasn't good.

With you I am home....

He remembered his five year old sister saying that to him after he'd found them shelter in an abandoned building, he'd found old rags and a large cardboard box for her to sleep in. He remembered her bright smile, with her two front teeth missing.

A smile he'd never see again because he'd failed to protect her.

He closed his eyes. *Evelyn help me.*

Why did you have me bring her here? What am I supposed to find? Why are you on that island?

Why would you conduct a mission without me? Without telling anyone? Don't you know how much...

Damian opened his eyes and sighed. He wished he'd never met Rosaline.

That he could forget the terrified then devastated look on her face when they'd first met; the soft curve of her neck when she'd turned her back to him; how she'd pushed the custard tart towards him; tenderly cared for Aidan; held her arms out wide to embrace him with the unspoken promise of sanctuary.

He'd pressed a knife to her neck, shoved her and she was still unafraid of him. He should have been thrilled, instead she unnerved him. What was wrong with her? What was it about those haunting eyes and that husky voice that made him lose control? He could feel anything but numb around her. Instead he felt too much.

And why was he thinking about his sister so much lately? Why would Evelyn have him bring Rosaline here?

He paused. Listened. He didn't hear anything. Perhaps Rosaline had left.

Stop being a coward, he could hear Lucas chide him. Evelyn would say even worse.

It was stupid to hide in his own place. That wasn't like him. He faced situations no matter how bad.

He would face this.

THE LINGERING trace of burnt paper greeted him as he walked down the hallway. Damian found Rosaline sitting on the dining table, swinging her legs with the boredom of a kid on a playground with no one to play with, a saucer with a tiny pile of ashes next to her. She jumped down when she saw him.

"I hurt you and I'm sorry," she said. "I didn't mean to. I don't say what I don't mean. So—"

Damian pointed at her. "Just drop it." He didn't even want to hear her say the word. Home was his father and brothers. That was it. He'd gotten more out of life than he could have imagined. He expected nothing more. It felt greedy especially since...

"And the reason I told you to hug Sandra was because she wasn't happy to see me here."

He remembered the anger Sandra had directed at Rosaline and how he'd been surprised by it. "She's not usually like that."

"You're special to her. She's used to having you to herself. She depends on you and felt threatened by me. So the hug helped to reassure her."

He narrowed his eyes. "How do you know this?"

Rosaline hesitated then shrugged. "Just a guess."

"No, it's not."

She lowered her gaze and rubbed her nose. "I get a sense about people." She looked up at him and held out her arms. "Ready for your hug now?"

He folded his arms. "I told you I don't want to hug you."

She walked up close to him and said in a low voice, "Because you want more."

He closed his eyes. "Do not tease me."

She didn't reply.

But she hadn't moved. He heard her breathing, smelled the scent of lotion she'd used on Aidan. *Reach out to me,* she seemed to say without words. *I'm here for you. I want to be with you.*

He gritted his teeth. He could feel her watching him.

"Do you wear makeup?"

He almost opened his eyes stunned by her question, but

he knew better, having grown used to her strange questions. He kept his eyes closed.

"It's just that your lashes are so—"

"I'm not wearing makeup," he ground out. His eyes had always been an embarrassing feature for him.

He felt her rest her hands on his shoulders then felt her rise onto her tiptoes before she pressed her lips against his neck. She touched his skin with the tip of her tongue.

His eyes flew open.

She smiled. That impish, tantalizing, dangerous, alluring yet innocent smile.

He narrowed his eyes and shook his head. "You shouldn't have done that."

Her smile grew.

He cupped her face and claimed her lips like a parched man stumbling upon a river of cool, fresh water.

His mouth slid to her throat and he released a growl of pleasure when he made her moan. He could devour her, feeling hungry for more, terrified by his passion and thrilled at her response.

Rosaline wrapped her arms around his neck, drawing him closer, pressing the soft curves of her body against his, making her desire for him known. He felt newly invigorated, as if anything was possible.

He was on fire.

And suddenly he heard an alarm. It took him a moment to realize it was coming from her phone.

Rosaline abruptly pulled back and swore. "I have to go."

His heart pounded; his words thick in his mouth. "Right now?"

She quickly checked inside her basket then closed the lid before she grabbed her coat from the closet. "Yes."

Damian stared stunned as Rosaline walked out the front door without looking back, swinging her basket as if leaving him standing there was the most natural thing in the world.

Then he felt the burning of his nails biting into his palms as his greatest fear came true: He watched her close the door without saying goodbye.

13

———

osaline had about forty minutes to savor the memory of the kiss, licking her lips with tasty satisfaction, surprised by how soft Damian's lips were, before she had to get her pulse back under control. She tucked the memory aside and pretended nothing had happened when she faced The Inquisitor.

"It's not like you to be late," her mother said meeting her at the door. A pinched faced woman with large glasses.

Rosaline hung up her coat.

Her mother glanced at the basket Rosaline had set on the ground. "Did you see your grandmother?"

"I went to visit her," Rosaline said. It wasn't an outright lie but she didn't want to tell her mother the truth. That she didn't know where her grandmother was and instead had found a beautiful, big black guy in her grandmother's bedroom. Such details were best left out.

"How is she?"

"Well enough," Rosaline said. "I didn't stay long." Also

sort of true. Once the hunters came they had left. "Come on, let's get you taken care of."

Rosaline followed her mother to the living room where they passed her stepbrother, a lanky teen who always managed to smell like ranch crisps. He managed the faintest nod in greeting, which wasn't a surprise since he barely acknowledged Rosaline unless he wanted to borrow money or to ask her to lie to his parents if she caught him where he wasn't supposed to be.

Her stepfather smiled when he saw her, and offered a feeble wave from his position in his favorite reclining chair in front of the TV. Rosaline inquired about his health, which was expected and routine, and he spent the next several minutes sharing all the ills he suffered, the doctor's visits and prescriptions.

Rosaline usually made him his favorite medicinal tea and massaged his shoulders. With effort he managed to make it to the horse races, sports events, the bar and back again, but steady employment was just too much for his poor body to bear so he spent most of his time in the same spot while his wife worked double shifts at a local hospital.

Not that Nayla minded. Work gave her purpose and with a daughter like Rosaline, she had few things to worry about. Rosaline not only made sure the housekeeper earned her keep, but that the fridge was sufficiently stocked and pampered her mother with foot massages and sensual bath oils. She was on her feet all day but in Rosaline's hands she felt as if she'd been floating.

Nayla looked down at her daughter as Rosaline dried her feet after treating her to a lavender scented soak. She had always been such an odd child. She worried about her.

While other little girls were bright and chatty, she was quiet but always willing to help as she did now.

Her two older siblings were busy with their lives and had little time for their parents after they'd gone off to university. Rosaline had stayed behind and Nayla always felt a little guilty. Nayla knew she depended on her daughter more than she should but liked the attention and felt as if she were doing her a service. Rosaline had never dated and Nayla doubted any man would have her. Or that she was even interested in them or anyone. She was almost glad she didn't. Who would want such a dark, solemn looking woman? One who barely spoke and preferred to stay by herself? She had a pleasant enough face but her eyes could be a little off-putting, which was why she'd trained Rosaline, since she was small to keep her gaze lowered.

"Have you thought about what I said?" Nayla asked her.

Rosaline kept her gaze lowered. "I'm not moving in with you."

"But you can't be happy living all alone in that strange little house of yours out in the middle of nowhere."

"I am. And it's hardly that," Rosaline said knowing her mother considered anywhere provincial that didn't have shops within five minutes drive, "It's easy for my clients to reach."

"Clients," Nayla said with a sniff. "I knew it was mistake to let you spend so much time with my mother." She stared at her for a long moment. "I don't want you to be alone."

Little did her mother know that even when Rosaline was alone she wasn't lonely. Rosaline loved her solitude and the house where she lived, it allowed her to not be overly stimulated by the bustled of suburban life—the school buses, the barbecues, the pool parties—the quiet helped her to concentrate. Her mother didn't understand the power of quiet.

But a stirring of worry began to build. What if Damian didn't? He lived in the heart of a residential district, what would he think of her simple lifestyle.

"Tell your grandmother to stop by. She never picks up the phone when I call her."

"I will."

"Are you sure things are alright?"

"They're fine."

"So you're not going to tell me what happened to your neck?"

Rosaline's hand flew there. She silently swore. She'd totally forgotten about her bandage. She'd barely recovered from her kiss.

"I wasn't paying attention and walked into a low hanging tree branch. Don't worry, I cleaned the cut and I'll be fine."

"I told you the woods were dangerous. I don't know why your grandmother is determined to stay there when we have plenty of space for her here. Stubborn as always."

"She likes her independence and it's a lovely little place. I know why she stays."

Her mother sniffed. "Two of a kind. Just promise me you won't get involved with any of the people she knows."

Her mother had used the same refrain as she had for years: *Your grandmother is not like other women, don't trust her people, they're not like us.* A belief Nayla had been taught by her father who'd raised her while her mother flitted in and out of her life.

"I can't promise you that," Rosaline said and before her mother could argue she said, "There's something I need to ask you about an island."

14

―――――

What the hell just happened?

Damian stared at the front door wondering if he'd imagined it all. Had Rosaline really kissed him like the world was about to end and then left without looking back?

Had she really come into his life like a whirlwind then left his life bare and empty?

Had he really let her into the private place of his life, let her seep into his heart only to let her leave him vulnerable?

He pictured his mother's back.

His sister's dangling, lifeless, arm as they carried her away.

Evelyn disappearing, leaving more questions than answers.

Was he doomed to being alone? He shouldn't have tried to hold on to her.

Damian picked up his cell phone then swore. He didn't even have her damn number!

You're not a stranger.

I know you'll find her.

With you I am home.

Damian calmly set the phone down on the coffee table. If he wasn't careful he would throw it.

This couldn't be it. She had to come back. She just forgot to tell him. Didn't she want to know what had happened to Evelyn?

Damian sat on the couch and took a deep breath. He told himself he wasn't staying there so that he could listen for her knock on the door.

He hugged himself and told himself he was okay, that his body wasn't really aching.

When he woke up at four in the morning, he told himself he didn't regret falling asleep.

He told himself she'd come back, that he hadn't been played for a fool.

But as he lay on the couch watching the soft rays of the sun grow ever deeper through the blinds, pushing away the darkness of night, he started to have his doubts.

Damian sat up and looked around the apartment, all remnants of Rosaline ever having been there were gone.

Fine. He was fine. He wasn't disappointed. Why would he be? Of course she wasn't coming back. Why would she? Finding Evelyn was up to him. He'd told her to leave. He was used to being alone.

But the kiss...

He rubbed his forehead. He wouldn't make a big deal out of that either. It was nothing. A passing moment of pleasure. Nothing more.

He checked his phone and Laura Metcliff's face appeared on the screen.

And the search continues although hope is starting to fade...

He released a low growl of frustration and quickly clicked away from the news report. He was not going to deal with someone else's heartbreak. He didn't want to think about another woman with eyes that haunted him. Rosaline, with her velvet voice, was enough. His focus had to be on Evelyn.

He took a shower trying to think of his next strategy.

He changed then sat at his dining table and called Shapiro and told him the status of things: That Evelyn had gone underground.

Shapiro sounded relieved.

He stood by the window and called Sandra to make sure Aidan was okay.

She told him he was fine. She had gotten rid of the items she had recently purchased just as Rosaline had recommended. Damian imagined Brendan would be just as relieved not to find the closet as stuffed as it had been, although Sandra had mentioned a cute pair of stuffed animals she'd seen online...

Brendan was fine too and would be back at home by that afternoon.

He sat on the couch and called his father to make sure he was alright.

The woman who answered his father's cell phone made it clear he was more than alright.

He went through his mental file to think if there was anyone else to call then thought of the bracelet Rosaline had shown him. He retrieved it from his coat pocket and stared at it. He rubbed his thumb over the wooden beads and began to count them—one, two, three, four, five, six.

He paused. Six? There should be eight beads.

He quickly counted them again. Onetwothreefourfivesix.

This wasn't his bracelet. He'd just assumed it was. It looked exactly the same, but his definitely had eight beads. He remembered Evelyn requesting it back when he'd outgrown it, telling him it was something she wanted to keep to remember him by.

But if this wasn't his bracelet...?

The ringing of his cell phone shot through his unease and confusion.

He glanced at the number and froze. Afraid to answer. He carefully set the bracelet on the coffee table, swallowed and then did.

"How are things?" his brother Lucas asked him. "You said you'd call me after you finished with Dad."

Damian sat on the couch and rubbed his eyes, feeling weary under the weight of his brother's concern. "Right. Sorry. Forgot." He gripped the phone and closed his eyes, breathing deep. *I don't know if I can do this. I can't keep pretending.*

"That's not like you. What's wrong?"

Wrong? Damian nearly laughed at hearing the word. Where would he start? Best not to tell him about the beauty with the shotgun or the two dead hunters. Or that he let Sandra into his private space and he'd kissed a stranger who left without saying goodbye and he felt as if his heart would burst. "Evelyn wasn't at the cabin. I think she went underground with a package. That's all I know." He wouldn't mention the map on the side of Evelyn's cabin, the biggest clue of all.

"Do you need me to—"

Damian sat back and closed his eyes, feeling some of his tension ebb. His brothers always reminded him that he wasn't alone. Both of them knew about Evelyn's organization and helped out in various ways. Lucas used his knowledge of architecture to figure out how a house was structured to hide people; he could spot a false wall, a hidden cabinet, an uneven staircase better than anyone. He'd once helped them find a child hidden in a trunk with two false bottoms. Lucas liked to joke that he'd learned building structure from being locked in his stepfather's basement for days on end, a statement that only made him laugh but one no one else found funny.

"Not yet," Damian said, "but I'll let you know."

"You sound grumpy."

"I always sound this way."

"She's going to be okay."

"Hmm. Yeah."

Silence.

Damian opened his eyes and said, "Lucas? Lucas, are you still there?"

After a noisy sigh his brother said, "I was doing my Ian impression."

In spite of himself, Damian laughed. Their taciturn brother always amused them.

"That's more like it," Lucas said, sounding pleased. "Now are you ready to tell me what's really going on?"

"I..." He paused, hesitated. Tugged at his sweater collar. "I've been thinking about my sister."

"Uh huh and what else?"

It hurt to admit it. "I messed up. I trusted someone I shouldn't have. Let them get close and now I feel like an idiot—"

"Is it the woman with the basket?"

"What?"

"The one you think you made a mistake with," Lucas clarified. "Sandra called me and told me about her."

Damian swore. He should have expected that. She had warned him she would.

"Yeah, got my hopes up and I shouldn't have. Won't happen again."

Lucas paused then said, "Do you remember that story Dad liked to tell us?"

"The one about the woman with the big eyes?"

Lucas sniffed. "It was big tits, man."

"No, it wasn't."

"Yes, it was. I remember it clearly. Never mind," he said quickly before Damian could argue, "the point is remember how she used to climb through windows and—"

"Dad never told me this story."

"Are you sure?"

"Very."

"About a woman who didn't speak much English but had a way with animals and was awkward and—"

Damian swore. "That was one of Dad's damn movies. *Rilinia the Elephant Queen*."

"Oh, yeah. You're right. Sorry about that. Are you sure it wasn't *Shana the Jungle Vixen*?"

"No."

"Okay. Anyway my point was—"

"You have a point?"

"Was that she made a lot of mistakes," Lucas finished. "But she still achieved her goal in the end."

"Are you actually trying to make me feel better using a plot point from a D-movie from the nineties?"

"Be fair, bruh, it was at least a B-movie." He paused. "Although if we were rating it based on the size of her chest—"

"I'm not having this conversation."

"It was definitely a—"

"Shut up."

Lucas laughed. "I find your innocence adorable."

"I'm hardly innocent. I really should go." He'd shared more than he'd wanted to.

"I'm being serious. From what I got from Sandra this woman seems special."

She was but not special enough to want to be with him. "As I've told you, I've been thinking about my sister," Damian said eager to change the subject.

Lucas fell silent then said, "Do you need me?"

It wasn't a simple question. Lucas would cancel his own surgery just before he went under anesthesia if one of his brothers was in trouble.

Although Lucas was the youngest in age, he'd been adopted first and had taken it upon himself to act as a big brother and welcome his new brothers into the household. Damian had been the second and Ian the last, all from different circumstances but quickly becoming a family, with friendly, helpful Lucas making it a seamless transition. He made it his aim to help Damian learn to read since Damian had barely spent a full year in school.

Every night Lucas would make sure they were okay and use a large flashlight to check for monsters who could be hiding under the bed or in the closet. Both Damian and Ian indulged their brother's nightly ritual knowing Lucas was more afraid of the possibilities of monsters than they were.

"No, not yet."

"Okay. I'll check in again later."

Damian disconnected then turned on the TV just for some noise and Lauren Metcliff's face appeared on the screen. He put it on mute then stopped.

She was missing and Evelyn had gone into hiding.

It could be a coincidence. But it probably wasn't.

They rarely dealt with high profile cases; it wouldn't look good for them. Most of their rescues went unnoticed, the right people were paid off to stay silent, the wrong ones were swiftly dealt with.

Could Evelyn have anything to do with this? Is that why she hadn't told him? It would make sense that a woman like Lauren Metcliff would have security detail.

Time to get some answers.

15

———

$\mathcal{H}$e called Shapiro. "I need a report on Lauren Metcliff. I'll give you until—"

"No, need. I can give it to you now. Evelyn had me look her up three years ago."

Three years! Why hadn't she told him that?

"What did she say?" Damian kept his voice neutral.

"I didn't think much about it at the time. There wasn't much to uncover and Evelyn seemed vague about the reason."

"How vague?"

"'I'm just curious' vague."

So there was the answer—the two cases were connected. Evelyn had taken someone others wanted to find. Others, who used the media, which most of their targets didn't, for various reasons. She'd taken a risk with an unpredictable person and done it on her own.

He heard Shapiro swear.

"What?" Damian asked him.

"I don't like this. How much trouble do you think she's in?"

"I don't know, but I'm not worried," Damian smoothly lied. "She's been planning this a long time. Tell me about Lauren."

"An only child. Degreed. Has a made-up position in her father's ironworks company..."

Lauren's life was so basic and boring Damian almost fell asleep listening to the details. There was no way if she hadn't been related to a wealthy family that wanted attention she would get any media coverage.

"Okay tell me about the husband."

"Evelyn didn't ask about him."

That was rare. Was it not a domestic issue they were dealing with? They usually looked at the spouse first.

"How about the parents?"

"I only did a cursory look," Shapiro edged.

"Don't care. Tell me what you got."

"Both parents came from money, when they split Lauren was around ten years old, the father got custody. He seems more adept at inheriting and marrying money (which he's done a few times) than earning it himself. He's known for hosting parties almost weekly. He's well-connected—has a couple top politicians in his pocket—and not someone you'd want to tamper with.

"At the time Evelyn requested the inquiry, her only focus was Lauren so I didn't dig deeper."

Why had Evelyn worked on a secret case without telling him? For three years?

"I'm sure she has her reasons," Shapiro said, answering Damian's silent question.

Was there someone she didn't trust?

"Yeah. Thanks." Damian scratched his forehead. "Um... has anyone contacted you?"

Shapiro laughed. "Got to be more specific than that."

"A woman...asking for a place to stay."

"No. Why?"

Rosaline hadn't called him. Perhaps she had somewhere else to stay. He hoped she didn't go home.

"You tell me about her and...I'll tell you something too."

"You've got more info for me?"

"You first."

Damian sighed. "Evelyn's granddaughter needs protection so I gave her your info."

"I thought she was going to stay close to you."

"What's the info you have?"

Shapiro hesitated. "I'm not sure but I think Evelyn's been driven underground by a third player."

He stiffened. "What does that mean?"

"When I sent our people to recycle the trash at the cabin, the raccoons had gotten there before us and the recycling was gone."

No bodies! That was impossible. "But they were there."

"I believe you. We watched them search, but they'd disappeared. The raccoons left empty handed. So who cleaned up?"

"And what scent had the raccoons followed in the first place?"

He hadn't alerted the raccoons, their code word for the police or other authorities, so who had? Damian closed his eyes and swore.

"Exactly."

Someone knew Evelyn wasn't there and was trying to set her up, but someone else was also involved.

"At least we know there's someone else looking out for her."

"Hmm." Someone he didn't know about was close enough to Evelyn to anticipate this? Who was this person and why hadn't they shown themselves?

"Don't be jealous," Shapiro said in a playful tone. "You know you're her favorite."

Damian frowned. "When were you going to tell me all this?"

Shapiro's tone turned sheepish. "I was hoping I wouldn't have to. That by the time I spoke to you again you'd have contacted Evelyn and she'd explain herself and everything would be fine."

"How do you live with such ridiculous optimism?"

Shapiro laughed. "In our line of work it's what gets me through. I think there's more good in the world than bad."

For some reason Shapiro's words stirred a tender place in Damian's heart—a place he'd still allowed hope to reside. A place that had made room for the memory of Rosaline's smile, her tenderness with Aidan, the sweet softness of her lips, the gentle gaze and her kindness to him until she'd taken it away. Damian shook his head annoyed at himself and his traitorous heart. "Right," he said in a gruff voice. "Keep dreaming. In the meantime, find out more about Metcliff."

"Will do," Shapiro said then disconnected.

Evelyn had given him enough clues to find her, but still he resisted. There had to be another way to uncover the mystery without going to that island.

Talking with Lucas and then Shapiro had given him some clarity.

The apartment where Evelyn stayed when she was in

town would be his next stop. He'd continue the hunt on his own.

But when Damian jumped in his Jeep minutes later, it didn't smell the same.

It smelled like damp earth, lavender with a touch of honey. And for the briefest moment Damian was swept back to the silent drive with Rosaline, who didn't ask any questions or offer any answers. Rosaline who only nodded when he motioned to the music display and let him choose what they'd listen to. Rosaline, who smiled and trusted him, which few people did. Rosaline, whose kiss was as sweet as blackberry jam.

The car shouldn't have smelled like her.

It had been hours since he'd driven her here. Damian paused when he heard a sound. He cautiously shifted his gaze to his rear view mirror and saw a prone figure in the backseat.

16

———————

The moist dark depths of the forest called her deeper. The known brightly lit path suddenly giving way to a dense tangle of brambles and tight canopy of trees. Pine needles whispered under her feet with each step and she saw her grandmother's cabin in the distance, but the forest was unfamiliar to her. The air thick with a pressing anticipation, the light buzzing of insects, the flutter of a bird. She should feel scared but she didn't. She kept going on, grasping the basket in her hand.

"Have you lost your way?"

Rosaline turned and saw an extraordinary man leaned against an oak tree. The low growl of his voice cutting through the silence. She noticed his broad shoulders, the intense gleam in his eyes. He smiled, flashing teeth that shone as white as polished alabaster against his brown skin.

She shook her head.

"Can I carry your basket?" he asked.

She shook her head again.

He took a step towards her. "Is there nothing I can do for you?"

Oh, there was so much. She could not read his aura, but his eyes told her all she needed to know.

"Rosaline!"

Her eyes flew open, the dream disappearing like smoke, giving way to hard, dark eyes simmering with anger. Damian's.

But it wasn't fear that made her sit up and gasp. It was his aura. It glowed with a red hot passion. He was on fire— illuminating desire so hot she had to resist stripping off her clothes and leaping into his arms.

"What is wrong with you!" he said, his words bursting forth like a primal roar. "Have you forgotten who I am? What I do? Do you know what I could have done to you?" He took a deep breath, lowered his voice. "What are you doing here?"

Rosaline remained speechless, caught up in the magnificent awe of his powerful aura, its tendrils licking the roof of the Jeep like colorful flames, spreading to the sides like the tentacles of an octopus. Yes, he was angry, but oh so much more.

"Rosaline!"

She blinked and swallowed. She briefly met his eyes then looked away. She held up her hands. "I promise I didn't do any damage to your–"

"I don't care about the Jeep!"

She kept her gaze lowered. "You really don't have to shout."

Damian exited the Jeep and slammed the door. When she didn't immediately follow he tapped on the window and motioned her out. Rosaline sighed and stepped out but before she could say anything Damian spun on his heel and marched back towards the building.

"Weren't you going somewhere?" she said.

Damian wordlessly held the door open for her.

From his aura she knew it was best not to ask any more questions. She walked to the elevator and pushed the button, glad he'd decided to return to the apartment since she needed to use the toilet.

"I didn't want to wake you," she finally said to fill the silence. It wasn't like her to do so, but the aura around him shifted with such an array of colors she had a hard time trying to pin one down. She needed to calm him. "I got back late after talking to my mother and visiting Nan's apartment. I asked Mom some questions then I contacted some names in Nan's address book. One friend said she was planning a trip but didn't say where. Evelyn tended to be vague about those things, but she went somewhere warm. The friend had seen what she'd packed and she'd needed a passport, so likely out of the country. I came back to tell you and I knocked, but...you didn't answer and...I didn't want to wake you."

Damian stared at her stupefied. "You knocked?"

"Yes."

"Are you sure?"

"No. I might have danced." She playfully punched him. "Of course I'm sure."

"I'm usually a light sleeper, I would have heard you."

"You were exhausted."

The elevator doors opened to their floor and he stepped out. "Still doesn't make sense."

Rosaline watched him fumble with the key to unlock the top bolt until he realized he was using the wrong one. Rosaline bit the inside of her cheek hoping he'd hurry up. By the time he opened the door she felt as if her bladder would burst. She shoved him aside and raced to the bathroom, making it just in time.

She washed her hands then her face before she freshened her breath with a finger toothbrush and some mouthwash she found nearby. An action she soon regretted. His mouthwash was so potent it made her eyes water and she felt like her gums would burst into flames and all her teeth would fall out. She scooped up some cold water to ease the burning and wiped her eyes.

When she felt suitably recovered, Rosaline left the bathroom and found Damian leaning against the front door with his eyes closed. He still glowed but the colors had dimmed to a powerful purple.

She cautiously approached him. "Are you all right?"

His eyes flew open and he pushed himself from the door. "You must be hungry." He folded his arms but didn't move.

She studied him, unsure. Did he expect her to make breakfast for herself? Fair enough. Rosaline started to turn but he took her wrist and forced her to face him before letting go.

He folded his arms again. "I didn't think you'd come back."

"I told you I would."

He frowned. "No, you didn't. You left without saying goodbye."

"Why would I say goodbye when I planned to come back?"

His frown deepened. "You didn't tell me you were coming back."

"Well I didn't spell it out, but I left a note."

He stiffened. "No, you didn't."

"Yes, I did."

"Where?" Damian looked around the living room. "I didn't find a note anywhere."

"Did you check the fridge?"

He stared at her. "What?"

"The note. It's in the fridge."

"Who leaves a note *in the fridge?*"

"Why are you shouting again?"

He waved his hands in frustration. "Because you're not making sense. What rational person puts notes *inside the fridge?*"

"Someone who's used to people who actually *eat* something. Did you have dinner or breakfast at all?"

Instead of replying, Damian marched into the kitchen and opened the fridge where he saw Rosaline's note on top of a covered plate. "Shit."

"You haven't eaten anything since yesterday afternoon? Are you on a hunger strike?"

He closed the fridge and mumbled, "I didn't think you'd come back," more to himself than to her then he pulled down a cutting board and began chopping a green bell pepper he'd grabbed from a container nearby. He took down a skillet and set it on the stove, continuing to mutter to himself, "A note." He shook his head poured some oil in the skillet. "Tell me more about Evelyn."

Rosaline stared unsure what to make of him then things became clear.

Now she understood. All the colors surrounding him, the searching look in his gaze, this feeling of surprise. He was used to being let down. He was starting to learn to trust. All the colors now made sense.

This was what joy looked like.

Pure, unadulterated joy.

She'd never seen it displayed this way before and it was the most wondrous sight.

She walked up next to him and stared in awe, covering her mouth as tears pricked her eyes.

He was happy she'd found out more about Evelyn. He'd been afraid she'd left him to find Evelyn on his own. He'd thought she'd abandoned him.

"Wasn't the kiss enough?" Rosaline asked, watching him sauté the peppers.

Damian's jaw twitched. "Are you teasing me again?"

She frowned. "No, I want to understand. I've never kissed anyone like that before. Why would you think I wouldn't come back? We're a team now, right? When will you start to trust me? I know how much Evelyn means to you."

He turned off the stove then faced her before he said very quietly and very softly, "This isn't about Evelyn."

17

———

She didn't know a man's gaze could glow like summer lightning.

Rosaline stumbled over her words surprised by the sudden change in him. His aura danced but his body remained eerily still.

"O-of course it is," she said. "You were angry because you thought I'd abandoned you in your search..." She let her words die away as she watched his energy shift. He slowly blinked then said in a soft voice, "This isn't about Evelyn."

Unease swept through her. Then what could the change in mood and atmosphere be about? Had she misread him? "But...you're happy that I'm here, right?"

Damian took a slow, deliberate step towards her. "Happy?" His voice cracked on the word. "I'm—" He stopped. Stared at her for a moment and then...

Oh! His lips were just as she'd remembered. And he whispered her name so sweetly and briefly, tenderly held her gaze before he kissed her again.

"I didn't think you'd come back," he said, his voice raw

with emotion. He searched her face. "Do you understand now?" he said and she nodded before another kiss left her breathless.

And at that moment she fell in love with him.

He was the one. She'd never have chosen him but now she couldn't imagine her lover being anyone else. His desire matched her own. She slipped her hand up his shirt, eager to feel the heat of his bare skin.

He drew back. "Let me make you something to eat."

Rosaline stared, surprised by the abrupt withdrawal. Food? He wanted her to think about food at a moment like this? "I'm fine. I thought you'd be hungry for something besides food. Aren't you hungry f—"

Damian pressed a finger to her lips. "Stop using that word."

"But—"

"I mean it." He kissed her then whispered against her lips in a low growl, "I could devour you, but not yet. Understood?"

Rosaline nodded then licked his finger like a naughty kitten. She hoped to convince him to forget about needing any food, but his eyes darkened with suppressed desire before he turned and continued preparing breakfast.

He wasn't used to joy, he'd grown used to denying himself pleasure. He'd learned to trust her but still didn't trust himself. She would slowly teach him that he didn't have to live under such tight control.

Rosaline sighed inwardly, silently admitting defeat. Maybe if she'd been more experienced it wouldn't be so easy for him to resist her. She followed him. "I can quickly make myself—"

"Sit down. This won't take long."

She hesitated, unsure. It was strange to have someone look after her. She was usually on the other end.

In minutes he'd made her scrambled eggs and peppers with toast. When he stood up to clean the dishes she said, "You have to eat something with me."

He stared at her for a long moment.

She boldly stared back.

He sighed resigned and put together the meal she'd left for him last night—another half of a tart, and another sub sandwich.

"How many of these did you make?" he asked her before taking a bite.

"Enough."

"Hmm."

"This place has a nice view," Rosaline said, just to be polite.

Damian shrugged. "I'm not particular. Any of the units would have been fine."

She frowned not understanding him. "Any of the units?"

He sat down in front of her. "Yes, it's no big deal since we own the building."

"But...I thought you worked for Evelyn."

"I do, but she doesn't pay me. I don't need the money."

Her gaze swept over his unremarkable sweater, it fit him well—very well—but was far from an expensive name brand and he drove a Jeep. A man like this could casually say he owned a building?!

She felt as if she were falling. He owned this fifteen story building? She'd thought she'd met someone who would be her equal. But no way would someone like him want to leave this spacious apartment to settle into the tiny house she had. The house she had no plan on leaving. Perhaps her flash about a future with him had been wrong. And what would happen when he found out about her ability with auras and flashes?

Her heart fell. She'd feared he'd upend her life but never considered he'd have to upend his to be with her. Such a change would be too much for him and unfair. She had so little to offer. Why would he want a lover like her? She had little experience and her income compared to his was laughable. Their lives were worlds apart.

She felt tricked. Weren't people like him supposed to drive expensive cars, live in penthouse suites that extended an entire floor with their own private elevators? Didn't they hire interior designers, display exclusive items they'd purchased on their world travels in curios dusted by maids? How could he look and live so normally?

And then there was the nightmare—or was it a dream?—of him tenderly holding her while covered in her blood...

"Is something wrong?" Damian said.

Rosaline looked up at him, startled. "Sorry?"

"You look upset."

"If...you're this rich shouldn't you have security or something?"

Damian ducked his head a little embarrassed. "My brothers and I live very low key lives so people overlook us." He paused. "No, scratch that. My brother Ian and I live low key lives, Lucas, on the other hand..." He left the rest to her imagination. He chewed his lip for a moment then said, "What's really bothering you?"

"I'm...I'm just thinking about Evelyn."

"You changed your mind?"

She blinked quickly. "My mind?"

"About me finding her?"

"No," she said quickly. "No, you will. Sorry, just drifting thoughts. Don't mind me." She focused on the food. "This is delicious. What do you call it?"

"Eggs and toast." His large hand gently covered hers. "What's upset you?"

I thought you were ordinary. I thought we'd have a chance together. I thought it would be forever. But none of that matters. She would savor whatever time she had with him and not burden him with her fears. Perhaps it was best they hadn't slept together. There were things about her that he'd find surprising and maybe—so that he wouldn't feel tricked—he should know things before things between them progressed any further.

It might scare him, push him away, but as much as it would hurt, perhaps it was for the best.

Rosaline bit her lip. He deserved to know the truth about her.

"I can see auras," she said in a rush, "not all the time, I have to tune into them, but it doesn't take much, and sometimes I have flashes about people or events that haven't happened yet. That's why I sometimes know more about people than they say. That's why I said you weren't a stranger to me. And I've had no feelings towards anyone until I met you and I thought you should know the truth so you know what you're dealing with and...why are you smiling?"

"Because this is the most you've ever said to me in one go."

"Oh, I'm sorry."

Damian shook his head with affection. "Don't apologize. I like it." He paused, held her gaze. "I like you."

"Even if I can tell you're hiding something from me?"

He sat back. "No, not then. That's when you scare me." He pointed at her. "Don't apologize. I'll have to get used to it." He folded his arms and pinned her with an assessing gaze. "What am I hiding?"

A challenge and test. She was ready. "That shape you saw on the side of the cabin was a map. I saw the same shape on Evelyn's desk. An island called Carliz."

He gave a brief nod for her to continue.

"You know that island, perhaps were born there. That marker on the map was familiar to you. You know where Evelyn is."

He shook his head. "I know where she could be."

"Then why are you hesitating?"

He lowered his gaze.

"Why don't you want to go back there? I saw a picture and it looks like a beautiful island."

His eyes captured hers. "A paradise warmed by the gates of hell." He stood, tapped the table with his finger, punctuating each word. "I vowed never to return. To think Evelyn would—" He turned and walked to the window.

Rosaline walked over to him. "There must be a reason."

"What reason? When did our relationship become based on lies?"

"She hasn't lied. I think she was protecting you and now needs your help." She took his hand. "You can do this." She held his hand in both of hers. "I can see how much you feel."

He frowned. "Why are you telling me this?"

"So that you know I don't care who you used to be, what you used to do. That won't change how I feel about you. It's time to stop letting the past define you."

Damian sighed resigned. "Do you have a passport?"

18

NEW YORK

*E*verett Metcliff once killed a dog with an iron skillet. It hadn't been intentional. He wasn't cruel after all.

He'd been trying to offer the dog a treat, but the dog turned its head away.

It ignored him.

And at eleven years old Everett didn't like being ignored. He didn't like that the dachshund seemed to favor his younger brother more than him. So that day he hit the animal as hard as he could.

He heard something break, like a cracked egg before the dog collapsed to the ground.

He watched as blood seeped from its nose and pooled at the side of its head.

He felt a little sorry.

But not sorry enough to tell anyone about it.

He made sure that the skillet and dog disappeared. He remembered hugging his brother as he wept when he told him that the dog had run away. He dutifully helped his brother put up posters around the neighborhood to help them find the missing dog.

They'd never gotten another dog.

He hadn't killed anything since then, but as Everett sat in his living room and stared at the owner of the private detective agency he'd hired to find his daughter, he wonder how long that would last.

He was losing patience. He'd paid good money for results and he wasn't getting any. "You still haven't a clue as to where she might be?"

"No."

The overpaid bastard didn't even look sorry, he looked bored. Ray Hardy came highly recommended but he was smug. He had an accent that screamed Lower East Side, although he managed to buy clothes farther West thanks to men like Everett. Ray wouldn't exist without him. Shouldn't the little piss ant be a little ashamed for failing him? But the man stood there, wearing dark sunglasses he didn't need, as if he didn't have a care in the world. "What's the hold up?"

"You went behind my back. You shouldn't have done that."

Everett didn't like to be told what to do, he always did what he thought was necessary. There was a reason men like him hired people like Ray—because there were winners and losers.

"If you have nothing else to report—"

"You sent two men without my knowledge. I told you not to do anything without my say so."

Everett tapped his finger against the arm of his chair. He felt it was necessary to hire extra help. He wasn't going to explain himself to anyone.

"But since you decided to get involved you must know

that your men got close to the target and then disappeared. Care to explain that?"

Everett pressed the flat of his hand against the armrest, his neck suddenly feeling hot as a seething anger grew. He hadn't known that. How incompetent could people be? But he wouldn't let the bastard know he'd been shaken, he wouldn't let him have that victory over him.

"She's gone underground," Ray added, stating the obvious with apparent amusement.

"I'll deal with it." He glared at him. "Why are you still here?"

"The money."

"What about it?"

"I haven't gotten it yet."

"I told you—"

"I know what you told me," he said. "I've been lenient. But you've upset me by ignoring my instructions. Makes me think there are things you aren't telling me."

"You know all that you need to."

"When I'm *paid* I don't ask questions. However when I'm not paid—"

"You'll get your money." Shit, he'd hoped to have found Lauren before he'd had to pay anything. He didn't have the money.

His business was in trouble and he'd burned so many bridges he was treading water in a dingy. But appearances mattered. His mother taught him that.

"You have by tomorrow."

"Or else what?"

Ray flashed a cold smile. "You don't want me to answer that question." He turned.

"Do you still have a son you want to see make it to college?"

Ray spun around.

Everett grinned glad to see the smug smile gone replaced by fear. He knew all about Ray's family and friends. What mattered to him, what didn't. He was one of those pathetic men who put family over money, which always proved a boon to men like him.

"You'll get your money when the job is done." Everett absently motioned to the door. "Goodbye."

Ray glared at him before he left.

Damn, arrogant bastard! Who was he to glare at him? And he'd dared to find out about the other team he'd hired? Who the hell—

"It's no use getting upset with him," Everett's wife said. His fifth and the most cunning. He hadn't married her for her looks since no amount of expensive creams and designer clothes could raise her above average (though she kept her brown skin supple and her figure fit), but she had money and a mind, which she used only to please him. He didn't need much more from a woman.

She'd been the one to alert him that his daughter might be up to something. He might have not noticed it if not for her. But he needed his daughter and the shares her mother had given her and the other assets he'd put under her name for strategic reasons.

If only his son-in-law hadn't been an imbecile. He'd chosen Casey Hayes carefully. How he could have messed up so badly was still beyond him. The well-dressed idiot still wouldn't tell him what had set his daughter off. He'd promised he hadn't said anything. That she didn't know anything about how well-orchestrated her marriage to him had been. Everett wasn't sure he believed him, although he doubted the overindulged only son of a business colleague had ever created or held a thought of his own.

"Did she find you with another woman?" Everett asked him. He had the kind of bland charm and features that women liked.

"No."

"A man?"

"No."

"You can't think of any reason why she'd disappear?" Everett said in an aggressive tone that usually made people tremble.

Casey shook his head, shivering a little to appease the hard snakelike gleam in the older man's gaze, determined to look as simple and dense as people expected him to be.

Lying to his father-in-law was the only way to survive. Most people underestimated him. Always had—from his hard driving father who made it his mission to remind Casey how much he was a useless disappointment; to his self-absorbed mother who bristled anytime he complained about his father's bullying; to his two sisters who fought to be their father's favorite using Casey as a battering ram to make their father proud, then there were the teachers who told him he was stupid, and the friends who pretended Casey was smart, stroking his ego with enough BS to make a field of flowers grow, so that they could help him spend his money. But he knew who to trust and who to betray.

He heard the slight trace of desperation in his father-in-law's voice. The one the media mistook for a father's care and concern. But Everett needed Lauren and Casey knew Everett hated needing anyone. He'd trained Lauren to be under his control, her disappearance was not only a surprise but a personal affront. Everett's ego couldn't tolerate disobe-dience, he also took her action as a betrayal. His father-in-law's pleas on social media had been in order to widen the search with the help of the public; he'd created a free army of soldiers of surveillance to let Lauren know that she couldn't hide from him. That he would find her.

But Casey would help to make sure that didn't happen. He'd been paid handsomely to help Lauren disappear. Unfortunately, he'd been foolish enough to fall in love with her; he'd pay the price for that miscalculation.

But soon he'd watch a towering figure fall while the skeletons in the Metcliff closet danced and that would make his sacrifice all worth it.

~

Maryland

Two days had felt like a year.

Rosaline thanked her driver, a sullen woman whose car had smelled like peppermint and onion rings, then got out of the car and stood in front of Damian's apartment building. It stood tall and arrogant, as if it could punch a hole in the icy blue sky, while a December frost froze the breath of autumn. A fierce breeze tugged at the hem of her jacket, causing her to shiver as she tried to gather the courage to see him again.

She'd left Damian's apartment after telling him she needed time to reorganize her schedule before she traveled to Carliz with him. In a few hours she'd enjoy the warmth of an island sun but for now she had to face this insistent chill.

We own this building. The thought of Damian's wealth still made her stomach churn. How could she make a relationship work with a man like this? She mentally shook her head; she didn't want to dwell on it.

Her cell phone rang.

"I'm sorry," Damian said once she connected, "Where are you?"

"I'm here. As planned. Is something wrong?"

"My brothers are here," he said in a grim voice.

How could he make his family sound ominous? "That's okay."

"They want to meet you," Damian said his tone becoming as grim as a funeral.

"Is...that a bad thing?"

He hesitated then said, "We'll see."

19

The Wolff brothers were not what she'd expected. They looked nothing alike and seemed as different as three types of plants—a cactus, bamboo and sunflower. But she sensed a fierce loyalty between them. Damian wasn't alone and she wondered if they would accept her.

She didn't have long to worry.

The sunflower brother, dressed in an expensive business suit that added elegance to his tall, slender frame, graciously took her luggage and coat and set them aside.

He flashed a smile as dazzling as a thief flashing stolen gems and introduced himself as Lucas. He wore his success without apology and Rosaline could imagine him driving a flashy sports car and walking into a party with a long legged model on each arm.

Usually a man like him would annoy her, but Rosaline felt herself being charmed in spite of herself. He had a powerful aura of strength and cunning that his gold wire framed glasses only hinted at. His hazelnut skin, handsome looks and charm was solely one way people would under-estimate him and he knew how to use that to his advantage.

But it was the bamboo brother, a silent man in the corner, sitting in a chair she hadn't noticed before, that caught her interest the most. He wore jeans and a dark green sweater, he had a rugged handsomeness devoid of polish or charm, but she couldn't help but notice him. His aura was so powerful it nearly filled every crevice of the room. She wondered how he functioned in daily life with such powerful energy. He didn't meet her gaze. He offered a quick acknowledgement before his attention returned to the book on his lap.

She wondered if he was shy or if it was a strategic move. Could he read her as well as she read him?

"It's no use," Lucas said noticing her interest. "He barely speaks."

"They'll have that in common," Damian said.

Lucas looked at his brother confused, but before he could ask him to clarify Rosaline walked over to the silent man.

Damian took a step forward to follow her.

Lucas blocked him with an outstretched arm. "It's okay."

"She shouldn't get near him without some warning. I've never seen Ian let anyone get that close to him before. She doesn't know who she's dealing with."

A quick smile came and went. Lucas adjusted his glasses. "She knows."

"I'm not sure."

"Let her be. You don't have to manage everyone. I've just met her and I can tell she knows what she's doing."

"What if he loses his temper?"

"He won't." Lucas rocked on his heels. "How did you meet her?"

"It's a long story."

"Make it short."

Damian made an absent gesture and said, "At Evelyn's cabin…I really think I should—"

"Leave them," Lucas said taking Damian's arm and leading him to the couch. "This should be interesting."

Rosaline remained unaware of the brothers' exchange—Damian's concern and Lucas' amusement—when she stopped a few feet in front of the third man. She noticed the large hardcover book filled with the fantastical illustration of a graphic novel.

His gaze remained lowered. She cleared her throat and said, "I'm sorry to ask. But does it still hurt you?"

He lifted his gaze and looked at her. She gasped. Beautiful, mesmerizing eyes met hers. She thought she'd be afraid. Such a powerful man. How could he have such a tender gaze? He was an observer like her. He could prove useful. He blinked. Shifted in his seat as if surprised she'd even approached him.

"Your leg," she clarified. "Are you in pain?"

He lifted a brow as if to say, You tell me.

She leaned forward. "May I?"

He shrugged.

She knelt and lifted up one of his pants leg, saw the brace. Winced at the scars. Then stared at the brace. True robotics. A marvel. She got lost in the design. Nearly forgot the man until she felt a light touch on her shoulder. She looked up quickly. "Oh, sorry."

She pulled the pants leg down. "It's amazing. You don't need my help at all. But I do have an ointment that might help you when you experience some pain from tight muscles. Would you be interested?"

Ian blinked then touched the side of his neck before he pointed to her.

"Oh this," Rosaline said with a laugh to ease his concern. "Your brother gave it to me. It's not much. Unfortunately, I scar easily like you." He narrowed his eyes. "No, it doesn't bother me at all. Truly." He lifted a brow. "It was partly my fault," she clarified. "I said the wrong thing to him. I know it's strange. He's not one to attack people. He thought I'd tried to poison him." Ian's brows shot up in alarm. Rosaline waved her hands and laughed at his outraged expression. "No, let me explain..."

From a distance Lucas and Damian continued to watch the pair, amazed. Lucas had taken a seat although he hadn't been able to convince Damian to do the same.

He took off his glasses, rubbed his eyes then put them on again. "I can't believe what I'm seeing. I've never seen a woman have that long a talk with him before."

"He still hasn't spoken," Damian said.

"But he's talking all the same. Careful you might lose your girlfriend. I'm kidding," he quickly added.

"I know."

Lucas sent a pointed look at Damian's hand. "That clenched fist tells me otherwise." He patted the seat cushion next to him. "Sit down, you look like you're about to abduct her."

Damian relaxed his hand and pushed down his jealousy but remained standing. Rosaline and Ian seemed to be in their own little world. Ian hadn't said a thing but he'd managed to make her laugh twice. A sparkling, beautiful sound. Soon jealousy revealed itself as fear. That perhaps

Rosaline wasn't meant for him. What if she'd met someone more suitable and similar to her?

Ian didn't open up easily. He shied away from people's pity. He didn't like the stares but he didn't mind Rosaline.

Lucas tugged on the cuff of his shirt. "She's special."

"I know."

"Can we keep her?"

"Shut up."

"You have nothing to worry about. But if you're really worried, all you have to do is flash those pretty lashes of yours and she'll be lost."

Damian sent him a cutting look.

Lucas placed a hand over his heart and feigned a swoon. "Be still my heart." He held up his hands in surrender and laughed when Damian's cutting look turned into a cold, angry gleam. "Relax. She only has eyes for you." He stood and rested a hand on his brother's shoulder. "We came by because I was worried about you. This," he nodded towards Rosaline, "is an unexpected surprise. Glad I got to meet her. Have you met Dad's new lady?"

"Not yet but I spoke to her on the phone."

Lucas folded his arms and nodded, his face grim.

Damian sent his brother a suspicious look. "What?"

Lucas shrugged. "Not sure. He's been seeing her for awhile but none of us have met her. He's been cagey about this one."

"Maybe he's not ready to introduce her to us yet. Might not be that serious."

Lucas rubbed his nose and patted his brother on the back, his grim expression disappearing like an ocean wave. He flashed a quick grin and said in a bright tone, "Maybe."

He shoved his hands in his pockets. "So, when do you leave?"

"Late afternoon. Plenty of time," he added when Lucas looked at the clock on the wall.

He paused then said, "Does she know?"

Damian rubbed the back of his neck. "Not everything."

"We all have a past, don't be ashamed of yours. And—" Lucas stopped when he noticed Damian stiffen. He turned to see what had caught his brother's attention and saw Ian closely examining Rosaline's neck. Lucas glanced at Damian's stricken face and made a loud whistle that caught the pair's attention. Rosaline turned, startled, and Ian looked at his brothers, flashing a devious grin that quickly disappeared when Rosaline looked back at him.

"We'd better go," Lucas said.

Ian slowly rose to his feet and Rosaline remained kneeling, looking up at him like a worshiper at the foot of a deity. Ian held out his hand and she rushed up to her feet and handed him his cane.

Lucas stifled a laugh, while Damian bit back a groan of annoyance. Ian slowly walked over to him, stopped, rested a hand on Damian's shoulder then patted his brother's chest as if to say, Lighten up, before he left.

"A pleasure meeting you," Lucas said to Rosaline before following Ian.

Rosaline said the same then rushed passed him and ran up to Ian. She motioned him forward and he bent down so she could whisper something in his ear. He patiently listened with his gaze lowered then lifted them and stared at Damian.

Damian mouthed 'What?' But his brother kept his expression neutral. Finally, Rosaline stepped back and Ian met her gaze and nodded, making her smile.

"What did you say to him?" Damian asked, closing the door after his brothers had gone.

"It's private."

"How can you have secrets with someone you just met?"

"I just met you and look at us."

Damian shook his head. "It's not the same."

"I'll tell you later," she headed to the couch.

He grabbed her wrist. "Why not now?"

She pulled herself free. "Because it's not important."

"It's important to me."

Rosaline sighed, searched his eyes then said, "Okay. I asked if you were keeping something from me about the island."

"Oh."

"But he assured me you'd trust me one day."

"He didn't say anything."

Rosaline smiled. "We both know he doesn't have to."

Damian paused. "He's an impressive person."

Her smile widened. She playfully tugged on the front of his shirt. "But I still like his brother more."

He shook his head. "There are things about me you—"

She looped her arm through his. "I told you, I don't care. You're an amazing man."

Damian bit his lip. "Would you still find me amazing if you knew I killed my sister?"

20

He'd meant to shock her and had succeeded. He had succeeded in a way he instantly regretted because he realized that as much as he'd wanted to push her away, he'd also wanted to hold her close. To see if she'd accept him. All of him. If she'd judge him as he'd judged himself all these years.

Damian waited to see the shock turn to horror and then curiosity. People were always curious about tragedy.

But Rosaline wasn't like others. He'd forgotten that. The shock in her eyes melted into sorrow and he watched, almost mesmerized, as tears gathered in her eyes then slowly slid down her cheeks.

In her eyes he saw compassion and understanding. Didn't she hear what he'd just said? When she reached out to touch his face he took a hesitant step back, as if afraid her touch might make him feel her anguish. He wouldn't cry, he'd emptied himself of tears years ago, but he would feel the weight of misery again.

He grabbed a box of tissues and handed it to her. "Don't cry."

She took a tissue and wiped her eyes. "I'm so sorry."

"Why?" he asked baffled by her reaction. "You didn't do anything."

She seemed impervious to his cool tone as her fingers wrapped around his hand in a gentle trap that kept him rooted to her. He didn't pull away, but also knew she wouldn't let him. "Tell me what happened," she said. "Or is that too painful?"

"Why are you crying?"

She held his gaze. "Because you're sad. So very sad."

He let his gaze fall, no longer able to look at her. She saw too much.

"Going back there is going to be very hard for you."

He nodded.

"That's why Evelyn wants me to go with you."

He closed his eyes. "What do you think of me?"

Instead of a reply, he felt her tugging him forward. He opened his eyes and let her lead him over to the couch. He reluctantly sat. Then Rosaline shocked him by sitting on his lap and rested her head on his shoulder. "Now wrap your arms around me and hold me like a teddy bear."

"No."

She sat up and stared at him surprised. "Why not?"

"Never owned a teddy bear. They scare me." When her lips quirked in amusement, he narrowed his eyes and pointed at her. "Don't laugh. I'm serious."

She bit her lip, quickly hiding her amusement.

"And why would I need to pretend you're a teddy bear anyway?"

"I wanted you to think of me as an object you could trust."

He gathered her close and held her snugly. "Okay."

"What am I supposed to be?"

"I'm not telling you."

Rosaline released an exasperated sigh but didn't argue. "Then tell me what happened. What was her name?"

He couldn't say it yet. Not out loud. Not after all these years. He couldn't say her name but he could tell her story. The story of a short, hard life.

"Our parents were out of the picture by the time I was six and she was four. But my best friend was a pudgy, baby-faced cross-dresser from the Philippines called Aunty Rico. I'd helped him when he'd first arrived on the island and someone tried to rob him and I jumped on the man like a rabid dog. Don't ask me why, I just did. But he never forgot. Aunty Rico and I were inseparable after that and he took us in without question." Damian didn't tell her how he used to enjoy watching Aunty Rico brush his wigs—something they were forbidden to touch— and how he'd lather their skin in sweet smelling lotions. How nice it felt to be touched and loved. He remembered once when Aunty Rico was smoothing cream on his face his friend looked worried and Damian wondered if he'd done something wrong.

"No, sweetie," Aunty Rico said with a bright smile that didn't last. "It's just. I worry about you. Those eyes of yours... Sometimes I wonder if I should..." The bright smile returned. "Never mind. It's nothing."

But he'd later learn it wasn't nothing.

"We stayed with him for a year," he told Rosaline, "until the night I woke up and found Aunty Rico standing over my cot holding a knife. Its tip glowed red. He promised me he wouldn't let them get me. I didn't understand what he meant, I screamed. He tried to explain that he wanted to save me, but I wouldn't listen. I didn't understand until years later after..." He took a deep breath. "Anyway I pretended to calm down and accept his apology then when he went to work I left with my sister and we ended up on the streets. But I found an abandoned building for us to stay in.

"My sister was sickly. Always had been, even as a baby. I earned money by gathering cans, helping tourists, and other odd jobs to make things work for us. I could have used the protection of a gang but decided against it, I turned down another opportunity as well.

"But then this cousin of mine told me about a medicine that could help. He was a street-wise type who always dressed well with ready money. He helped me out every once in awhile so I trusted him. He said the medicine wasn't too much, that he wanted me to work for it so that I wouldn't get used to expecting charity. I worked hard and it took me nearly two months to raise the money. I skipped meals, took in extra work. I remember handing him the money and taking the little brown bottle he'd given me. I felt like I'd been given gold.

"I rushed home that day and told my sister that she was going to get well. I gave her the medicine and she coughed a little bit, made a strange face and then she smiled.

"I left her to get us some food. There was a street vendor who would leave some remnants out for us, but she wouldn't stay around long enough to protect it from animals or others as desperate as I was, so I had to hurry.

"When I returned, she was still in the makeshift bed. That wasn't like her. I could hardly keep her in one place.

"I walked over to her. She looked awake, but she didn't blink...she didn't move.

"At first I wasn't sure what I was looking at. It didn't seem real. How could she be like this?

"I said her name, shook her but she didn't reply. Her eyes glassy, her body limp. In a panic I found my cousin. He came, saw her and told me I'd given her too much.

"It didn't make sense to me because she'd only taken one swallow. I saw her. But perhaps when I'd left her she might have taken more. It didn't matter. It was too late. I couldn't wake her. She was gone." Damian fell silent. He stroked Rosaline's arm, taking comfort in her warmth desperate to combat the coldness creeping over him.

"My cousin said that he wouldn't tell anyone what I'd done if I...I worked for him. I didn't want to. I'd resisted for so long. At three years old I remember my father punching a man who'd offered to buy me in exchange for the rent money.

"In my panic I went looking for Aunty Rico. It was at that moment that I finally began to understand why he'd wanted to mark my face. Why he'd said he wanted to protect me. But when I went to his apartment he wasn't there.

"I learned a rival had put him in the hospital and he'd left the island with the nurse that had cared for him. With no one left to turn to, I felt I had no choice. My cousin told me that even if I didn't get sent to prison, because I was a minor, he'd tell the town what I'd done and who'd want to hire a murderer? He promised to keep my secret. My shame."

"How long did you work for him?"

"About eighteen months."

"You were a child."

"Doesn't matter. It's one moment I regret. My sister trusted me and I..."

"And you've been punishing yourself since."

"If only it were that simple. Sometimes I think the secret ate me up more than the act itself. I've been hiding for years. Now I have to face myself. I wonder why I didn't just throw myself into the sea and join my sister in death? What life was I trying to protect?"

Rosaline slid off his lap. She sat beside him and cupped his face in her hands. "I'm glad you lived. Think of all the good you do now."

"It doesn't feel enough."

"Life isn't transactional. It's too complicated. Every chance you get to do good you take it. That's all any of us can do."

Damian bit his lip. "How can you...still look at me like that?"

"Like what?"

"As if I'm not a monster?"

She let her hands fall to her lap. "Because I see monsters all the time and you're not one of them."

Damian closed his eyes because her words soothed him and he was afraid to believe them.

"I saw a monster once," she said her husky voice seeming to penetrate the darkness he'd sunk into behind his closed eyes. "I was about nine or ten and was sleeping over at a friend's house when her older brother came into the room. He didn't know I was there. He'd been away at college. Didn't know she'd made a friend like me because others didn't like her much. She usually smelled like unwashed clothes and had a habit of stealing your lunch when she didn't think you noticed.

"But I noticed her and I befriended her because..." Rosaline bit her lip. "There was something about her, I felt I had to." She leaned back against the couch and stared at the black flat screen.

Damian squeezed her hand impatient. "Well?"

She blinked as if coming out of a spell. "Well what?"

"What happened? You said you saw a monster and then what?"

"Oh, right. Um...where was I?"

"You were sleeping over at a friend's house." Damian paused as a thought struck him. "Are you making this up? Is the friend really you?"

Rosaline shook her head. "No, it wasn't me. It really was a girl I'd met. The brother didn't know I was sleeping in bed with her when he came into the room and...I didn't always talk like this. I made him really angry that night..." Rosaline glanced down at her nails with grim satisfaction... "I stopped him, attacked him with all the fury my little body could muster." She let her hands fall to her side, his voice growing soft. "But he was stronger and he choked me, breaking a vocal cord. I had to have surgery. So... I know what monsters look like. I've met them and you're not one."

Damian felt the blood drain from his face. He thought of the scar he'd seen on her neck, thought of the wound he'd left with the knife and yet...

She'd offered him redemption. She'd freed him from his internal fear. The reason why he'd kept people at a distance. She wasn't offering platitudes that most people would: Those well meaning community workers on the island who'd never known desperation; who pinched their nose at the stench of suffering that surrounded them; those who ignored his father's pleas for work, after a factory incident had left him with the use of one arm, while they catered to the whims of tourists; those who were willfully blind to the systems of hierarchy and inequality as long as their bellies were full.

He'd managed to climb out. He could mimic their poses, but he could never forget what life had shown him.

That there were actions he could never take back.

Rosaline hadn't given him excuses and explanations (you were young, you didn't know, etc...) things he'd told himself millions of times that didn't ease the guilt, instead he knew she'd seen and experienced the darkness too. That there was always a price paid. He could only trust others who had also faced the darkness of life.

She had seen a monster, and declared he wasn't one.

Damian stared at her surprised she could still smile, still be so kind after what she'd endured. He hadn't managed to do that. It was as if something inside him had died, but she'd rekindled it. He wasn't a monster.

He believed that. In her gaze he saw a new man reflecting back at him. He saw the man he could become, one not haunted by the demons of his past, one who dared to love again.

But before that man could take hold...slowly...ever so slowly...a cold fury began to build, he was angry that she too, as a child, had been so cruelly treated...

"Give me a name," he said, his voice laced with the soft promise of vengeance.

Rosaline shook her head. "You don't need to fight my battles."

"What is his name?"

"You mean 'was'."

"He's gone?"

"Yes, he can never hurt someone else again." She

touched the rigid line of his jaw. "Don't take on my pain. Let us live in the moment, right now. We survived. We're alive."

He didn't move, but she watched the expression in his gaze darken with desire, smelled the scent of hunger.

And Rosaline read the look in his eyes and understood its meaning. "We might miss our flight and—"

He captured her lips, making it clear he didn't care.

21

Yes. This.

Rosaline's sweet mouth seemed to soothe the war within him. Conquering the rage, fear and disgust. He didn't want to go back to that wretched island.

Damn three years of secrets.

Damn puzzles and messages.

Damn the dark memories of his past. Let him savor this moment.

He was being reckless, careless, selfish and for the first time in his life he didn't care. He wanted her.

Damian rose to his feet, reached out his hand to her. "Come on."

She hesitated briefly, but enough to make his heart constrict. He couldn't bear her rejection now. But before he could say anything, she jumped to her feet and ran ahead of him then he heard her laughter floating down the hall.

He felt his wounded heart leap to life, filled with hope before he raced after her, easily reaching his bedroom before she did.

Rosaline stepped inside the expansive room, a soothing white, cream and grey, then turned to him, for a moment looking unsure. He motioned her to him with a crook of his finger until she was close enough, then he undressed her with exquisite care eager to enjoy each moment. She shed his clothes next with the same care until there was nothing but a hairsbreadth of distance separating them.

He'd been naked before but he'd never felt this bare. This exposed.

Damian turned to the bed, ready to ruffle the pristine sheets, but Rosaline took his hand and slowly sank to the ground, gently tugging him down with her.

The action startled him but before he could protest she wrapped her arms around him, enveloping him in her intoxicating scent, letting him indulged in the soft give of her breasts, the feel of her warm breath against his skin.

They both descended into the buttery soft embrace of the plush carpet.

He gathered her close, feeling her tremble. He became half possessed unable to bury the hunger any longer.

This time when he kissed her it was with a greedy demand. Eagerly. Shamelessly. Ravenously.

He savored how readily she responded to him, almost dizzy from the heady scent of her arousal and yet...

something...

was off...

Damian paused as a sobering realization struck him. "You've never done this before." It wasn't a question.

Rosaline bit her lip, a look of guilt and worry briefly crossing her face. "Is that a problem?"

Damian felt himself starting to panic. He'd never been somebody's first before. He'd made sure not to be that important to anyone so that he wouldn't be responsible for their feelings There were things she didn't know and he didn't want to shame or embarrass her. His mind raced, recalling how rough he'd been with her.

The only time he'd taken any care was when he'd slowly undressed her, but after that he'd been almost wild. His gaze swept over her bruised lips, thought of how when he'd first grabbed her how her body had trembled. He swore and sat up.

If he'd known he would have taken his time, but she seemed so willing, eager, and confident. Nothing he did seemed to shock her.

"Please don't stop," she said, sliding her hand down his thigh. He grinned at her naïve attempt, then saw uncertainty and wounded pride flash in her brown gaze and let his grin fall.

She trusted him and he didn't want to lose that trust. He lifted her in his arms and whispered, "I don't plan to," before he kissed her and placed her on the bed. When she sent a longing glance to the carpet he chuckled and said, "Next time," before covering her sweet, swollen lips again.

This was different. Not only was he a first for her, but she was a first for him. The weight of her expectation and way she looked at him with complete surrender was both thrilling and terrifying, intoxicating and sobering. He didn't want to mess this up.

He kissed her neck then said, "Do you mind if I...instruct you a little?"

She frowned. "You don't like what I'm doing?"

He hesitated searching for the right words.

She smiled. "It's okay. Go on, tell me what you want."

"If you relax and trust me," he said slowly parting her

legs, the soft whisper of shifting sheets highlighting his words, "I think you'll like it too."

She shrugged nonchalant. "I already like it but...Oh!" she cried out in surprise and delight when she felt the solid pressure of his fingers as they slid inside her and settled in a key spot. She squeezed her eyes shut in sweet agony. "W-what are you doing?"

"Don't think about what I'm doing. Do you like it?"

"Yes, but I think--."

"Don't think. Enjoy it."

"B-but this isn't how it's done."

He laughed deep in his throat. "It's only one of many ways."

She opened her eyes. "But what about you? You can't be enjoying this."

His gaze swept over her body. "I am," he said in a low growl. "I'm enjoying this very much."

It wasn't a lie. He'd never felt more himself than in that moment. She didn't judge him against others; he didn't feel as if he had to perform. No matter what he did, she accepted him as he was.

"Come to me, Damian."

"I'm here."

"I mean all the way."

He took a deep breath. Briefly closed his eyes.

Don't think. Don't think. Don't think.

He slid on a condom and then entered her with a bit more eagerness and speed than he'd planned to, but when he swore at his blunder, she laughed and held him close.

He didn't have to fear her rejection.

There was nothing to fear at all.

It was an intoxicating feeling.

He was used to being rated, like horseflesh, from partners who only cared about their pleasure and never his. In his late teens and early twenties, when the memories of his youth had overtaken him and he hadn't thought he'd deserved better, while also craving someone's touch, he'd offered himself to people who'd treated him like an object until he'd learned to distance himself from that toxic need and others.

He'd been starving so long he feared he couldn't get enough, that he would overwhelm her, but every time he started to pull away she held on.

Delirious joy swept through him.

And with every action he claimed her until he had to surrender to the realization that she was as much his as he was hers.

He bit back the words 'I love you' it was too soon for that. Instead with every gesture he said, 'Be mine.'

And she replied, 'I am.'

And soon he pleaded, 'Take me.'

And she replied, 'I will.'

And the aching loneliness dissipated...for both of them.

Rosaline never imagined it could be like this. This lover of hers knew every touch her body craved, he needed no instructions, taming her hot flames of longing with a cool confident command, his large hands cascading over her body in sensual exploration while inside he shattered every memory of pain.

But he continued to surprise her, because although he was a big man with big hands and big brown eyes with dark lashes, she'd never imagined how long and big his tongue would be.

And how well he'd use it.

How it would leave a warm, wet trail across her faded scar, a tongue that slid down her side and made her feel like the most delicious and delectable dessert. And even how it would explore her most intimate of places until she felt he would devour her.

He whispered a word.

But it wasn't a word she'd ever heard before. A foreign word that needed no translation it's meaning clear in the language of lovers.

He held her tenderly, sweetly, but when she drifted off to sleep it didn't stop the recurrence of the nightmare.

The nightmare where he was covered in her blood, followed by a fear that she'd lose him.

Rosaline shot up out of the nightmare, gasping for breath, her skin sticky with sweat.

"Are you okay?"

She bit her lip, feeling guilty. "I'm sorry, I didn't mean to wake you."

Damian rested a hand on her back, his voice soft. "That's not what I asked."

Please don't let me lose this. Even for a moment. She fought to control her breathing. She couldn't remember the last time someone had truly worried about her as a person not because she was different and considered strange but because they cared about her.

She didn't want a relationship were he felt he had to worry about all her gifts. Knowing she saw auras were enough, that's all he needed to know about her...bad dreams and flashes were a little too much too soon.

She couldn't tell him. She couldn't tell him that something horrible might happen. She would survive this. She always survived and there was a reason Evelyn had wanted her to go to the island with him.

"I'm fine," she said. "Just a bad dream."

He studied her for a long moment then cupped her face. "Nightmares wake me up too sometimes. Want to tell me about it?"

Never. Perhaps it was only a nightmare. Maybe it wouldn't come true. Maybe it represented something else. "No. I want to forget it." She slid back down, snuggled close to him. "We'll have to reschedule our flight."

She felt him stiffen.

"You can go back there now. You're ready and I'll be with you."

She felt him take a long deep breath.

She felt confident he could go back to the island of his youth free of the ghosts of his past. She only hoped she wasn't leaving one nightmare to face another.

22

———————

Few would have guessed that the large, handsome black man in first class had ever taken shelter in a cardboard box. They'd managed to get another flight the following day and would reach the island in the afternoon.

Damian looked casual in jeans and a grey T-shirt that seemed solely designed to show off his broad shoulders and biceps. Rosaline watched in awe at the casual confidence with which he presented himself, feeling as if each encounter with the outer world, beyond the forest, further widened the gulf between them.

Damian Wolff was far from the stranger she'd found lurking in her grandmother's cabin. The forest felt like years ago instead of only days.

His aura was that of a hunter as they sat in the luxurious private car that had picked them up from the airport and navigated through the picturesque streets—lined with colorful 17th century buildings. Rosaline wasn't sure whether to stay close or keep her distance. Damian was on edge; again, he took no pleasure in anything. She saw him cast his gaze on everything with a guarded suspicion.

The city's bright island colors in hues of yellow, pink and blue mingled with Baroque architecture and postmodernism hinting at the various influences that had made their impact over the centuries. One side street reminded her of the quaint tranquility one would find in a village of a Grimm's fairy tale while the looming presence of a cathedral made her shiver as if she were in the presence of Count Dracula's castle.

On the drive, when she'd thought Damian was lost in thought, he'd taken her hand and said, "Are you okay?"

For a moment she panicked, wondering if he worried about her ability to see auras, that being in crowds could be difficult for her. She was careful to mute her senses with sunglasses and a large scarf, which she could use to cover her face and head if necessary. She'd had to do a lot of planning for this trip so she wouldn't give herself away; she didn't want to be a burden to him, but then realized it was a simple polite question. She smiled and said, "I'm fine. Are you?"

"I'm trying to be." He squeezed her hand and let it go, turning his face to the window, allowing for no more questions.

But she sensed torment; he was in a private battle and not winning. She tried to distract him.

She pointed. "That church is impressive."

Damian glanced at the structure, wishing he could see it through her eyes, instead he felt himself go cold inside.

"You can visit anytime," their driver said.

Damian glanced away. He knew the large cathedral prided itself on its open doors while it closed its eyes to all that happened just outside.

He saw a person taking a photo of themselves in front of a brightly colored building, two children raced passed carrying bags that rattled with the sound of bottles.

So much had changed since he'd left and yet nothing had.

The tiny island was a dot in the Caribbean Sea and too small to cater to a larger tourist flow but had plenty of beaches and hotels with balmy temperatures to lure a few hearty souls who cared more about leisure than culture.

However, the island had a shadow industry buried deep under the shade of the palm trees, masked under the gentle moonlight that glistened over the sea at night.

No one would know what really went on as they walked along the clean roads bracketed by street food vendors. The fancy carriage rides that took tourists around the main section downtown cleverly distracted from the reality of what happened on the outskirts and within the heart of the city.

The island appeared so bright and cheery. Everyone, visible for the tourists to see, looked so happy—it was part of the allure and illusion and paid for by the unlucky few, like him, who'd been forced into the underground sex trade.

Damian thought of the desperate choice he'd had to make. His father had left when he was five. Not on purpose, he'd gone out for a drink with friends and gotten mowed down by a drunk driver. His mother hadn't coped well.

One night she smelled like honeysuckle, gently stroked his face with her bright pink fake nails touching his cheek and said, "Be good. I'll be back soon." And never returned fortunately he had Aunty Rico to turn to.

Nearly a year later, while collecting bottles, he saw her downtown, getting out of a posh car—shiny chrome, black wax finish. She spotted him and pretended not to see him. He'd hardly recognized her in the slinky silver dress, gold earrings and draped on the arm of a portly businessman, who owned one of the clubs Damian had once overheard her tell his father that she'd be a star in one day.

Damian followed her, knowing he only had one slim chance to get her attention. He ran up to her and pretended to accidentally bump into her before he said, "You dropped something, Miss," while keeping his fist closed so that she couldn't see that it was empty.

The businessman began to brush him aside, but his mother whispered something in his ear and the man disappeared into the restaurant. His mother grabbed his arm. He noticed the fake nails had disappeared, they were now manicured with frosted tips. She led him to an alley that smelled like booze and rotten fruit before she shoved him against the wall.

"This is my chance and I'm not going to let you ruin it," she said. "He has the connections to make me a star. His father used to work in the movies." She tapped her chest. "Could you imagine me on the big screen? But I don't mind starting small. Bit roles and the like, you know. I'll work hard. You'll see. I'm not going to be tied down because I made a stupid mistake with a man who wasn't worth it."

"Dad was a good man," Damian said defensive, still missing him although it had been nearly two years since his passing.

"Goodness doesn't get you anywhere," she spat out. "See where it's gotten you? What has he left you, huh? Nothing. I'm not going to be loyal to a memory and neither should you. When I make it, which will be soon, I'll send some money your way."

She didn't ask where they were living, how they were coping, if they'd eaten that day. Her unasked questions hanging between them like a foul smell. "What are we supposed to do now?" Damian asked her. "She needs medicine."

"No point. She won't live long."

Angry tears burned his eyes. "Liar."

His mother shrugged. "I've lived a lot longer than you. Even in the wild animals know to abandon the sick. You're too good." She sighed. "I'll see if I can get a job for you in one of the shows or..."

She cupped his chin, an ugly smile marring the beauty of her face. "There are plenty of ways to earn money on this island, dearest. Too bad you got the looks your sister should have. With lashes like yours you could do very well."

He jerked away from her.

She looked down at his meager pickings. She shook the bag with pity. "Or you can starve." She turned and he remembered how his skin burned where she'd touched him, how the click of her high heels echoed down the alley as she walked out of his life again. He remembered how the sun touched her brown skin when she stepped out of the shade of the alley into the bright light of the main street. How the sway of her dress reminded him of a snake hunting for its next meal. How alone he'd felt.

The betrayal still stung.

"She has to survive," Aunty Rico had said to him over a plate of spicy fish and yellow rice when Damian bitterly told him what had happened. His wig was gone, but he hadn't washed his face so his brown eyes appeared extra luminous highlighted with rhinestones and red eye makeup but hours later the makeup would be gone too when he appeared by Damian's bed that night grasping a knife...

Damian jumped when he felt a hand slide into his. He heard a deep husky voice whisper, "Stay with me."

He'd drifted too far into the past. A dangerous place to be. He turned to Rosaline and found solace and comfort in her gaze. He gave her hand a squeeze. "I will." He cleared his throat.

He stared straight ahead. He didn't want to see the kids on the street remembering that he'd once been one.

The car stopped in front of an awe inspiring palatial hotel, surrounded by palm trees.

Damian took a deep breath. The X on the map had led them here. And night hadn't fallen. He could get through this and let the sun warm the coldness that clung to him. The mystery of Evelyn and Laura would soon end.

23

At the reception desk, while Damian waited for the clerk who profusely apologized before dashing off to help a junior with a more demanding customer, Rosaline excused herself to go explore the gift shop. In no particular hurry, Damian rested against the counter, turned and caught the eye of a young boy.

He knew that look. He knew that he only had to make a gesture and he'd have him for the afternoon (maybe even the evening) for the right price. Things had changed since he'd left. The hotels were usually off-limits. The government used to be very careful not to mix the two businesses but economic desperation and a tinge of greed had blurred the lines.

Damian quickly looked away. But he could feel the boy's burning gaze on him or was it something else? Damian silently swore, straightened, then motioned him over.

The boy swiftly closed the distance between them, his feet silently crossing over the hotel's cream colored porcelain tiles. Damian pointed to the luggage and the boy dutifully picked them up.

A man, probably in his late twenties, flaunting an expensive haircut and trim mustache, khakis and a silk shirt with cream colored shoes (that looked impractical but stylish) joined them and spoke to the boy in French before he looked at Damian and said, "What are you doing?"

Damian just looked at him, careful to keep his expression blank the way Evelyn had taught him, trying to assess his next move.

"English?" the man said.

Damian almost responded in French before he realized that would be a bad move. He knew the man was referring to the language rather than the region so he tried to decipher the next best move. He could pretend to be a reticent Brit, self-deprecating Canadian, overly sharing American or friendly Australia. He'd played all those roles in his life. He hadn't thought much about the identity he would wear. He decided on a West Coast American and flashed a broad guileless smile, trying to appear as open as the Pacific Ocean.

"It's my first time here," he said, leaning against the counter once more and sounding casual, as if they were old friends. "It's a beautiful country and has so much to offer. Do you know anyone willing to show me the sights? Oh, and I'm sorry if I stepped on any toes. See, I have a bad shoulder and I thought this kid could help me."

The young man hesitated and Damian could feel him assessing Damian's clothes (which he'd chosen with care—from the designer jeans that signaled his income status to the color, cut and fit of his T-shirt) wondering how he could make a catch of him for himself. Damian guessed the younger man had likely been in the game a long time and had aged into rent boy status but likely had a way with managing the younger ones, so he'd been forced into another position that put him in charge. It was a longer lasting gig but it didn't hurt if he also wanted to put himself forward and make extra money for himself. "There are porters for that."

Damian discreetly flashed a wad of bills then slid it into the young man's khaki pocket. The trousers were so tight he had to use extra force to get the money inside. "I'm sure there are."

Greed lit the man's eyes. "I have younger."

His empathy for the young man disappeared. Damian swallowed. If he wasn't careful he was apt to kill somebody. He held the man's gaze, careful to keep his smile in place, careful not to also encourage him. He knew the young man would try to get information from the boy later on and may appear at his door and try to come up with his own arrangement. This was survival after all. He was likely not being watched by the organization, but Damian couldn't risk showing his hand and offending him either. "I'm sure you do," Damian said, keeping his voice neutral and disinterested.

"Sir?" the hotel clerk said, coming to his rescue, "thank you for waiting."

It was a cue for the man to stay silent and he remained so as Damian resumed checking into his hotel room, knowing the man was paying attention to key details like the hotel number and floor. Once he was finished he said to him, "It's been a long flight. Excuse me," and walked past him.

He saw Rosaline, her sunglasses hooked on the front of her brightly patterned blouse looking like a happy tourist. He caught her eye and shook his head. They could not appear to be together or his plan wouldn't work. She halted confused, but to his relief didn't approach him. He glanced in the direction of the lounge and she nodded understanding he'd meet her there later.

Damian entered the elevator and took the luggage. The boy gasped in alarm.

"My shoulder healed quickly," he assured him. "You don't have to do anything." He hoped to make it clear he didn't expect anything from the boy except his company.

The boy quietly followed him to his hotel suite. Damian opened the door, set the luggage down then motioned him forward. "Wash up then eat something." He motioned to the fruit bowl he'd ordered that now sat on the dining table. "I'll be right back."

THE HOTEL SEETHED WITH DESIRE, delight, innocence, danger, greed, and desperation, touching every corner with palpable raw human emotions.

Rosaline did her best to balance her awareness of the energy surrounding her but it wasn't easy.

She wondered why Damian had changed when she'd returned from the gift shop, but the man he'd been talking to had a dark presence and the child had an aura of fear.

Rosaline spotted Damian coming into the lounge. A casual observer wouldn't notice anything, but she saw a quiet anger that radiated from him when he approached her. She rose to her feet alarmed. "What's wrong?"

"I did something stupid," he ground out between clenched teeth, "and I'm starting to regret it." He sighed. "Let me show you to your room."

She laughed.

He frowned.

She blinked. "You're not joking?"

"Why would I be joking?"

She playfully tugged on his shirt. "Why would I need a separate room?"

He cleared his throat, lowered his gaze. "I-I made reservations before...um..."

"You discovered I was a sex goddess?" she teased him.

A hint of a smile. "Right, before then." He rubbed his chin. "I don't think I'll be very good company while we're here."

"You'd rather be alone."

He shook his head. "No, but—"

"I can handle the different sides of you. I have them too." She rested a hand on his chest, felt his heart racing. "I know being here is hard."

"Hmm."

"Promise not to kill anyone."

He bit his lip and she sensed her teasing ease some of the tension in him. "Fatally wound? Mortally injure?"

She shook her head. "No."

"Incapacitate?"

"Perhaps."

He released a long breath. "Okay."

"Cancel the room. I'll sleep on the couch."

His gaze met hers. "Not an option."

"Please, can we just go upstairs now? We'll discuss everything there."

"Okay, come on." He cancelled the other room reservation and paid the appropriate fee then led Rosaline to their suite.

He walked into the sumptuous suite scented with the

subtle fragrance of jasmine, lily and lemongrass, surprised the fruit bowl on the table was still untouched; he felt the faint tendrils of lilac scented steam as he walked past the bathroom. He saw Rosaline halt at the bedroom door then quickly back out.

"Um...Damian..."

"Yes."

"That mistake you made? What do you plan to do about it?"

He looked at her confused then saw her cautiously shift her gaze to the bedroom.

24

———

"No, no, no, no, no!" Damian said, rushing into the room.

He became a man possessed, quickly gathering up the child's shabby clothes and tossed each item on the bed one by one while speaking rapid fire French.

The naked boy cowered against the headboard.

"Damian," Rosaline said, "Calm down. You're frightening him."

But he didn't stop. He kept speaking and gesturing to the boy until the child's eyes filled with tears.

"That's enough," she said.

Damian ignored her and asked a series of questions, tossing them like bullets, making the child wince each time before he quietly replied.

Damian gestured to the window. Rosaline lost her patience and punched him hard in the side. He grunted and glared at her. "I said stop it," she said in a firm voice.

He rubbed his side. "You couldn't just say so?"

"I did but you weren't listening."

He rested his hands on his hips. "I'm listening now."

But Rosaline was done talking. She was ready for answers. A lot of them. She shot a glance at the boy.

Damian's hands fell to his sides. "I can explain."

"Which part? The naked child or the reason why you were terrifying him?"

"I wasn't...I thought I made it clear..." Damian sighed turned to the child and said something to him in a gentler tone.

The child still stared at him wide-eyed.

"Does he speak English?"

"He probably understands it better than he can speak it."

"I can speak it, yes," the boy said.

"Good," Rosaline turned to Damian. "Give us a minute." He hesitated then left.

The young boy began to relax. "I am for you then, yes?"

It took Rosaline a moment to realize what he meant. He thought Damian had bought him for her. "Oh, no," she said horrified then realized she sounded as if she was rejecting him. "No," she said again softening her tone. "Um...we just want—"

"Me to watch you? I quiet in corner, yes?"

Rosaline gripped her hands together not wanting to know why a couple would get off on a child watching them having sex. She cleared her throat and shook her head. "We just want to talk—really. Just talk," she emphasized when he narrowed his eyes, curious. In his world 'talk' could be a euphemism for something else. Heaven only knew what he'd been asked to do in his young life, "with you because we have no children of our own. I'm sorry he scared you. He didn't mean to." She stood. "Please get dressed."

"You are sure...?"

"Very sure. Please get dressed. Then meet us in the other room."

Although he stood completely unselfconscious about his nakedness, Rosaline turned to give him privacy.

She closed the door and walked into the living room where she found Damian staring out the window.

"He's getting dressed," she told him.

"And you didn't stay to watch?" he said in a broad British accent. He clicked his tongue. "You prudish Americans."

"That's not funny."

He dropped the accent. "I'm not trying to be funny."

She stood beside him. "Have you calmed down?"

"No." He shoved his hands in his pockets and sighed. "I shouldn't have lost it like that. I'm sorry." He folded his arms. "He looks twelve but he's only ten you know."

"Was that one of the questions you asked him?"

"Yes."

"What were the other ones?"

He fell silent.

She rubbed his back. "They're only memories, they're not your life anymore."

But they still felt so real. Memories of hands everywhere. He'd been deemed a 'candy': sweet, pretty, light. Something a patron could fondle and pleasure themselves at the sight of, but never penetration. That was the dominion of the ones deemed 'pincushions.'

He knew he'd been lucky—only outercourse and nothing too rough, he'd been carefully monitored—but he remembered the feel of grasping, eager, needy hands, hot breaths and cold fingers, sweat soaked skin pressed against him. And if they tried to go too far...

"He's ready," he heard Rosaline say. She gently touched his cheek. "It's okay now."

He'd done another reckless action, still not sure of the consequences but he knew there'd be some. He looked at the boy and saw his past staring back at him. It wasn't okay yet, but he'd make it so.

Rosaline pulled out her cell phone. "It's a long shot, but I'll try anyway."

25

———————

She showed the boy a picture of Evelyn. "Have you seen this woman?"

The boy shook his head.

Damian took out his wallet and said to Rosaline, "Information comes with a price," before handing the boy some money.

The boy carefully tucked it away then said, "She comes to the...um..." He looked at Damian and said something in French.

"The hotel bar and club?" he said.

The boy nodded. "Yes, she is a strange lady."

"Why do you say that?"

"She forgets so many things."

Rosaline and Damian shared a look. That didn't sound like Evelyn.

"How?"

"She will lose her way or leave things behind, but she is kind so..." He shrugged.

"We can see this woman at the club now?"

"No, not now. Later. When busy."

"We're getting somewhere," Rosaline said optimistic.

But there were still more questions.

"Thank you," she said to the boy. "Are you hungry?" She pointed to the fruit bowl. She placed a paring knife with a carved wooden handle she'd bought at the gift shop on the table next to the bowl.

He shook his head.

"Then go and watch something."

He sat on the couch and turned on the TV.

"He's lying to you," Damian said. "You're taught to never say you're hungry. We might as well order something for all of us."

"Oh, is that why you don't like me to say you're hungry?"

He glared at her. "No."

She bit her lip to keep from smiling. "I see."

He sighed and shook his head. "No, you don't. Now about the club—"

"We'll wait until evening, there will be more people then. I can go alone. It'll be okay since it's inside the hotel. This island is affecting you more than you thought. Trust me on this."

"No, I'm fine."

It was only when she gently took his hand that he realized he was shaking. He pulled away and rubbed his forehead, ashamed.

He was supposed to be stronger than this. "Something feels wrong about this." He rested his hands on his hips. "But it's a lead and I want to follow through. No, don't look at me like that. This is not a discussion." He picked up the hotel phone. "What would you like to order?"

"I've been here before," she said in a quiet voice. "You're not the only one with a tie to this island."

He stared at her startled. "You have? When?"

"A long time ago when I was with Evelyn. It was a strange trip. My mother didn't really want to come and my sisters complained because they'd wanted to go to Disneyworld. I remember thinking that Gran was distracted.

"I remember thinking it strange that there weren't many other family's like ours. Lots of couples and groups but not kids."

"How...long ago was this?"

"Twenty something years I think. Mom was so upset because Gran didn't return with us. She said she had something to do."

Could his rescue and her visit have overlapped?

They ordered a light meal and treated the boy to a pineapple tart before they prepared for their evening excursion.

26

———

Children were not allowed in the club during certain hours so their young guide had to try to sweep the area from the doorway.

"She is not here," he said.

"Maybe if we snuck you inside?" Rosaline said. "What do you think Damian? Damian?"

He blinked and cleared his throat, his tongue heavy in his mouth. He tried not to gape at the dark skinned beauty standing beside him, letting his gaze linger on the black long sleeve sheath dress that gently emphasized every curve of her body, the black velvet choker that graced her neck, cleverly concealing her scar. Rosaline's stunning transformation left him speechless. He'd always found her attractive but he'd never imagined this when he'd ordered the dress for her. It completely overshadowed the plain oxford shirt, dark jacket and trousers he wore.

She frowned. "Are you okay?"

The boy shook his head before Damian could reply.

"Sneaking is no good," he said rejecting her suggestion. "She is not here tonight, maybe later, yes?"

Rosaline nodded, sending Damian a quick, curious glance before she said, "Yes. Tell us the table where she usually sits."

"Sits?"

"Yes, when she comes to the club where does she stay?"

The young boy threw his head back and laughed. "She does not sit. She cleans."

"Cleans?" they said in unison.

"Yes, she is very good and clever when not forgetting things. You barely notice her, the guests don't, the manager don't, the owner don't, but I notice her because she is kind."

"Thank you." Damian gave him more money. "You have been very helpful."

His face fell. "You have no more use for me?"

"Why don't I take him back to our room just for another couple of hours?" Rosaline said.

Night had settled over the city and changed its vibe. They both knew what awaited the boy once they let him go but Damian suddenly felt uneasy. "I'm not—"

She took his hand and squeezed it as if sensing he didn't want to see her go; didn't want to be alone at the club without her. "You can look for Evelyn. She might show up later." Rosaline brushed her lips against his, briefly pressing her body against him in an achingly sexy promise of pleasure, before she said, "Don't worry. I'll be back," then took the boy's hand and left.

THE CLUB HAD A SLEEK, urbane feel of a bygone era, he half expected Edith Piaf or Adelaide Hall to appear on the stage. While smoking wasn't allowed indoors, the club held a hazy scent of cheap and expensive colognes and perfumes which mingled with the aroma of different wines and liquors as it floated through the dimly light atmosphere barely camouflaging wanton displays of lust.

Damian sat down at one of the booths, careful to avoid the gaze of the woman softly moaning as she squirmed on her date's lap, his hand so far up her skirt it took little imagination to know what they were up to. He ordered a drink and did his best not to remember Rosaline's alluring scent and the feel of her body against his before she'd walked away; he only briefly imagined how quickly he could get her out of that sheath dress when the time was right.

Thinking about her made him feel less alone, made him not fear the shadow world that thrived at night. The world he'd once belonged to.

The stage set up—excellently lit, pristine platform, professional background, modern acoustics—was better than he'd imagined giving the club a charm he hadn't expected. He leaned back, wondering if the performers would live up to the decor and nearly choked on his drink when the first performer sauntered onto the stage and stood in front of the microphone.

An older woman in a low cut, shimmering red dress.

A woman whose back he'd seared into the memory of his mind.

Damian slowly set his glass down and leaned forward unable to believe what he was seeing.

Age hadn't done much to alter her beauty but life had, hardening lips and eyes that had once bloomed with promise and dreams, now crushed like a dried rose kept between journal pages. Its fragrant scent only a memory.

Her voice floated through the club and landed on him like snow, melting the moment it hit him to be forgotten once he left. Everything about her performance was serviceable but unremarkable. He felt his heart constrict in pity and that filled him with rage.

She'd given up her children for this? Was this the fame she'd been craving? The limelight she thought she deserved?

He wanted to look away, but continued to stare, mesmerized, wanting to despise her, but feeling his pity only grow. She moved the same way, smiled the same way, as if nothing had changed. As if she was still a young woman on the brink of being discovered. She looked like a sad reflection of herself. It wasn't that her beauty had faded but that it had proven useless for her and one terrible day she would realize it. Perhaps in another decade or two, but it would be a cruel moment.

When she finished her set, Damian meant to look away, he knew better than to catch her eye, but he didn't. Instead, like a bullet piercing with lightning speed through space, their eyes collided. She blinked; he swallowed, his heart pounding with the weight of a sledgehammer.

He still had a chance, an infinitesimal moment, to break their gaze, to look away, to back down. But he didn't, holding his gaze for an extra beat, coming to a decision he hoped he wouldn't regret.

He discreetly called her over. She spoke to the crowd then made her way over to him, her lithe figure sashaying every step of the way.

She quickly assessed him—costing out his shoes (briefly frowning at the style but impressed by the brand) and his suit (a simple cut made with material that could set her back six months' rent)—before she sat down and smiled. "Did you have a song in mind?"

"No."

She slid close to him and he fought to keep his expression neutral, determined not to reveal how it sickened him that the scent of her desperate, hungry chase to catch the right man to ensure her way to a better life, still lingered. Did she ever think of them? Did she know her daughter was dead? Had she even shed a tear? Did she care what had happened to her son? Did she ever try to send money to him? Was there no maternal love there?

Damian felt the heavy weight of her hand sliding up his thigh. He stiffened and shook his head. "That's not why I called you over."

The welcoming smile fell as she quickly assessed his sexual preference in a new light. "If you prefer bananas to peaches—"

He gave her the once over to appease her wounded ego. "That's not it."

Hope returned to her eager brown gaze. "In the right light I look younger and I can move—"

"No," Damian said quickly not wanting to hear her elaborate. He removed her hand. "Not that either."

"Then don't waste my time."

He slid her a few bills. "I didn't plan to."

She tucked the bills away.

"You don't recognize me, do you?" he said.

"Should I?"

Considering how much she said he looked like his father he thought she might have. At least his eyes hadn't given him away, he'd been afraid—perhaps a little hopeful—that they might have.

There was no point dredging up the past. He'd made it out. He'd made a life for himself without her. Let her keep the dignity she had left. He didn't know if the man she'd dumped them for was still around and he didn't care.

"No," he said flatly.

She slid out of the booth and turned her back to him. This time when she walked away he didn't feel anything.

He reached for this glass with a sense of relief then realized that Rosaline hadn't returned. He'd been so distracted at seeing his mother again that he hadn't noticed.

He pulled out his cell phone and texted her. When he didn't get a ready reply, he stood to leave.

He wouldn't worry. He might panic a little but he wouldn't worry. She wouldn't disappear like Evelyn had.

He headed for the exit, taking one last look at his mother, who was smiling with two older men, offering her a silent final goodbye. She was one ghost from his past he could finally bury.

He left the club ready to head back to his hotel room when he felt a chill race through him.

He'd felt the chill of awareness before.

Someone was watching him.

27

———————

*D*amian swiftly turned and noticed a stooped figure, dressed as a hotel maid, disappear into a crowd of newcomers, eagerly entering the club anticipating a night of drinking, entertainment and whatever else money could buy.

But he was tall enough not to lose sight of her as her shuffling gait quickly became more assured and fluid. She turned a corner and made her way down into a stairwell.

He nearly lost her in the basement, the uniform grey walls and floors reminding him of a maze, but soon caught sight of her again as she turned into the laundry room.

The place was oddly empty...almost as if she was leading him somewhere.

He cautiously opened the door, felt a vise like grip ensnare his wrist. But he knew that move and quickly slid out of it, facing the woman he'd been searching for.

A maroon colored cap hid her hair, with large glasses obscuring her eyes, but he recognized that strong chin and powerful movement.

"Evel—"

"What the hell are you doing here?"

He opened his mouth then closed it unsure of how to respond. His relief turning to confusion.

"You're not supposed to be here," she said.

"Why wouldn't I be here? You wanted me to be. You...sent me clues."

"No, I didn't."

Damian thought of the boy's assessment of her that she was forgetful. Could it possibly be...? He tapped his chest and said softly and slowly. "Do you know who I am?"

Evelyn frowned and said in a warning tone, "Someone who knows better than to treat me like a child. I haven't gone senile. I didn't send you clues. I'd never have you come back here."

His mind raced, that didn't make any sense. "But...your chair...the hunters...the bracelet. I saw it, but it's not mine. Whose is it?"

Evelyn narrowed her eyes suspicious. "What are you talking about?"

"Even the ivy growing on the side of the cabin. Rosaline figured that one out."

Evelyn held up her hands. "Wait, wait. You met Rosaline?"

"Yes. At your cabin. We've both been worried about you. What were we to think when we hadn't heard from you in over a week and now I find you here dressed like this? What's going on?"

"Rosaline was at the cabin?"

"Yes. She came with me."

Her brows shot up. "She's on the island too?"

He nodded.

Evelyn rubbed her chin and swore.

"What's wrong?"

"I'm not sure yet," she mumbled.

He pulled out his cell phone.

"What are you doing?" Evelyn asked, watching him typing a message.

"Trying to get a hold of her. She was to meet me in the club, after returning a boy to our room." Damian waved his hand, stopping any questions. "It's a long story. But she hasn't shown up yet and hasn't responded to my texts."

Evelyn swore again.

"Tell me what's going on."

"I've already said I'm not sure yet." She opened the door and looked out into the hallway then left, motioning for him to follow her. "You can't be seen down here. "What room are you staying in?"

"How did you guess I was staying here?"

"Just a hunch," she said but he guessed she knew more than she was telling him. She opened the door to the stairwell. "What room?"

He gave her the number.

"Okay, go there and wait for me." She held up her hand when he opened his mouth to argue. "And I'll explain what I can."

"But I have to find Rosaline."

"Trust me, we will. But for now I need you to go to your room and stay there. Don't leave."

"Are you in danger?"

She hesitated before she said, "No."

"Do you think Rosaline's in danger?"

Evelyn shoved him forward. "We don't have time to waste," she said before hurrying down the hall.

He softly swore, the lack of response telling him all he needed to know.

He returned to his room and halted at the sight outside his door.

A different man, with a preference for attractive brown skinned women with blonde highlights in their shoulder length brown hair, would have welcomed the sight of such an attractive woman waiting outside his hotel room.

Damian wasn't that man. He scowled and pinned her with such a dark look the woman's tentative smile faltered.

He moved passed her and keyed the door. "I think you have the wrong room."

She adjusted her square shaped glasses. "Aren't you Damian Wolff?"

He opened the door in no mood for whatever ploy she was trying to pull. "Who's asking?"

"His sister."

28

———————

*P*unching a hole in the wall was his first thought.

His second was to walk inside the hotel room and slam the door in the woman's face. He chose neither.

Instead, Damian closed the door very carefully and counted to ten.

He wasn't in the mood for this. He wasn't in the mood for another hustle. But perhaps this could get him answers to where Rosaline was. Someone knew more about him than they should have and he'd figure out who.

He leaned against the wall, attempting to appear annoyed but unfazed. She couldn't know she'd rattled him. He tucked away his anger and said in a neutral tone, "Damian Wolff doesn't have a sister."

The woman stared up at him, the pulse in her neck prominent, she was not used to this, but she still held his gaze. She was nervous but unafraid. He admired her courage. "No, but Damian Bouchard does."

He tugged on the cuffs of his jacket to keep his temper in check. He'd underestimated her.

Damn she was good. He should have suspected it. Of course his mother had recognized him! The family resemblance was strong after all, huh? She'd put it all together at last and had quickly come up with a scheme. This was the game she was going to play? She'd hired some stranger to get money out of him not knowing that her daughter was dead? Foolish, desperate woman. He wondered how much it had cost her to get the right information about him.

He had to admire his mother's ingenuity even if it seemed a rather elaborate game to play. But her scheme wasn't the most logical. What bothered him most was how vaguely familiar this woman seemed. She had a vulnerable and fragile air (it hadn't been easy to dismiss her). His mother must have gotten a hell of an actress to play this role and take advantage of a sore spot. Fortunately, money always made it go away. "How much do you want?"

She frowned confused. "Nothing."

"Just name your price so we can end this charade."

"I don't need your money. Do you know who I am?"

God she was good. She really did look surprised and hurt. Why did she seem so familiar? He studied her a little more and saw the shape of her mouth and eyes. The hair was different as were the glasses and he assumed the freckles had been hidden by makeup, but he finally placed her. "Lauren Metcliff."

Her face brightened. "That's right."

"Are you enjoying your little disappearing act?"

"It's not like that. I—"

"Don't know, don't care." Damian opened the door and stepped into his hotel suite.

"Evelyn told me where to find you."

He gripped the handle. No, this can't be! His sister was dead! Evelyn knew this.

"It really is me," Lauren pressed when she saw him hesitate. "We can take a DNA test—"

It was a lie. A bluff. He closed the door. He needed space to think. But there was no chance for his mind to rest as his gaze frantically scanned the room for the barest of signs of where Rosaline could be. He noticed an orange missing from the fruit bowl, which had been there when they'd left, so it looked like the boy, Rosaline or both had made it back here. Plus, the lights were still on, causing the large windows to appear like large black rectangles as they framed the night sky.

Rosaline. Where was Rosaline?

"We named the fleas!" Lauren said, her voice muffled by the door but no less urgent.

He swung the door open without thinking.

He'd never told anyone that. Ever. His hand shook; it was too wild to believe. This couldn't be real. He stumbled back, swallowed as Lauren slowly, carefully made her way into the room. "It's impossible," he finally managed in a raw whisper. "My sister is dead. I saw her die."

"No, I survived. If you'll give me a chance, I can explain."

He shook his head, continuing to move away from her. "It's impossible."

Lauren lifted up her sleeve and showed him her arm. "I got this scar when I got splashed with hot oil when we were racing through the marketplace. We'd stolen some fried bread."

"But I gave her—"

"A drink," Lauren said. "That tasted a little bitter."

"And she stopped moving."

"Because it left me paralyzed, unable to respond, but I was still alive. It was terrifying. I could hear you but I couldn't move. I couldn't scream out. I couldn't do anything. I remember our cousin's laughter as he and someone else put me in a van, it wasn't a pretty sound. I remember wanting to cry but being unable to. I remember being taken away and then given to this woman with a sweet smile. She gave me something to reverse the effects of the poison and told me that I didn't have to be afraid that she'd help me to become stronger and that you'd be coming soon, but they had to take me away first because of—" Lauren took a deep breath. "Because you wouldn't have come otherwise and they wanted to help us both. But you didn't come."

Damian shook his head, confused. "But how did you become Lauren?"

"The woman with the sweet smile was right, I did become stronger. Strong enough for me to work with other children carrying bricks on a grand plot of land. She told us that we were helping to build a school. Our school. I was happy because I knew how much you wanted to go to school. I couldn't wait for you to come.

"But as days turned to weeks, I heard whispers that it wasn't really a school but her second house. I learned that the sweet smiling woman's eyes could become as hard as marbles when I asked about you, or didn't carry the quota of bricks I was supposed to. Or if I helped another child who'd fainted in the hot sun.

"Months passed and I was miserable. I missed you and every day brought more bricks, more tedious repetitive work. Then one day, almost with glee, she told me...you were dead.

Killed like Daddy was. By a car. But before I could shed a tear she introduced me to this well-dressed man and told me he and his wife wanted to be my parents and take care of me so I wouldn't have to work. I was so unhappy and sad that I agreed to go with him. He took me far away from here and changed my name.

"But I never forgot you. Never stopped thinking about you." Lauren took a hesitant step forward. "I never imagined you'd grow up to be so big."

Damian slowly fell to his knees, the weight of his anguish making his words barely coherent. "I thought I'd killed you."

Lauren knelt in front of him, wrapped her arms around his neck and held him close. "But you didn't."

He closed his eyes surrendering to the warmth of her embrace before he whispered the name he'd been unable to say, "Carin."

"I thought I'd never see you again," she said in a choked voice. "I can't believe this is real."

Neither could he. Damian drew back and gazed at her. Really looked at the face that had been so hard to look at when it had appeared on his phone or on the flat screen, flashing across the news. Now he saw his sister and knew why the freckles had felt so familiar.

He chewed his lower lip. "The media reports said you needed medicine. Are you—"

"I'm fine," Lauren said with a cynical laugh. "That lie was Everett's way of making my disappearance more exciting."

"I'm sorry you had to go through that."

"It's okay."

"So...You forgive me?"

"Oh my dear brother," she said with a teary smile, "there

is nothing to forgive. How could you know you were dealing with such dangerous people? We were tricked. You always looked after me, protected me, loved me. Thoughts of you got me through so many dark days."

He searched her face thinking of the reasons she'd had to contact Evelyn in order to disappear.

He'd worked with Evelyn to help spouses escape dangerous situations before but this—a public disappearing act—was a new one. And Evelyn never sent the people to him after a rescue. Most rescues would be put with the right contact and then Shapiro would help them recreate their lives elsewhere. She could have revealed herself to him then. Why now? What had triggered this change?

He was afraid to ask why she'd had to run. He didn't want to hear that her husband had hurt her in anyway. If he had, Damian knew there were ways to make him pay. But he couldn't dwell on that right now.

He had to figure out why Evelyn had kept Lauren a secret from him (and what was taking her so long anyway??) and what had happened to Rosaline.

He rushed to his feet, his words interrupted by a knock on the door.

29

———————

a stooped, shuffling figure walked into the room when Damian opened the door. Evelyn tugged on the jacket of her uniform, her disguise still in place.

Although she looked like an unremarkable hotel staff worker, her voice was cool and commanding when the door closed behind her and she looked at Lauren and said, "Did you tell him?"

She nodded.

"Why didn't you?" Damian asked her.

Evelyn walked over to the couch and sat. "Tell me about Rosaline." It was just the kind of non-answer he'd expect from her.

"What is there to tell?"

"Did she tell you about herself?"

He began to ask her what she meant, then he paused as a thought came to him. *I know you will find her.* Not 'we' but 'you'. Rosaline had never indicated that they'd find Evelyn together. It had always been just him. As if she knew something would separate them.

Damian felt his blood go cold.

Had he been wrong all this time? He'd thought about Evelyn telling him she hadn't sent him any clues. Most of the ones, except for the chair, Rosaline had uncovered.

Rosaline had noticed the vines on the cabin, the hunters' boots, even the bracelet (that he'd assumed was his and wasn't) and the voice recording had been sent to her.

She was the one lured to this island, not him. She'd been the target all along. But the target of what?

"Tell me what you're thinking," Evelyn said, taking off her cap. "Do you know...about her gift?"

"Yes, she told me about seeing auras and having flashes."

"And do you believe her?"

"Yes, but—"

"Excuse me," Lauren interrupted.

"Not now," Evelyn said.

Lauren cleared her throat. "I'm sorry, but—"

"Who else knows about the cabin?" Damian said.

"No one," Evelyn said then paused and he saw a secretive, worried expression cross her face.

"What is it?" he pressed her.

"Probably nothing."

"Two hunters showed up at the cabin and were swiftly dealt with—both disposed of by someone and taken away by someone else. That got Shapiro thinking."

"Shapiro knows—"

"He's just as confused as I am. Someone is out to hurt you but someone else wants to protect you. Someone who seems to know a lot more about you than we do."

Evelyn held his gaze for a long moment then said, "You have to go. Get off this island." She looked at Lauren. "Both of you. You can get a flight…" She let her words fall away when Damian folded his arms and shook his head.

"I'm not leaving without Rosaline," he said.

"That's not what I need from you right now."

"I don't care what you want. I'm not leaving here without her."

"Rosaline isn't your concern."

"Yes, she is."

Evelyn's eyes narrowed. "Do you still want to work for me?"

A threat like that would have made him pause in the past. She meant so much to him and the thought of losing her, losing an identity he'd struggled to build by rescuing others, would have terrified him before. But not now. The Evelyn in front of him felt like a stranger.

Damian let his arms fall to his hips. "Three years. You kept a secret from me for three years."

"I have my reasons and I'll explain later," Evelyn said with remorse, "but right now I think you're both at risk. If someone's gone after Rosaline they'll go after you too."

"Who else knows about the cabin?"

"This isn't the time for questions!"

Lauren held up her hand with a timid boldness. "I'm sorry, but I really think—"

"What aren't you telling me?" Damian demanded.

"A lot!" Evelyn said exasperated. "I've lived a long life. Done a lot of things. I have a past. A past that might have caught up with me. This isn't the time for me to tell you about it." She took a deep, steadying breath. "You've gotten what you've always wanted." She gesture to Lauren. "Your sister. It was a mystery I've been trying to solve for years. The bracelet was for her. I kept them together on my dresser as a reminder that I had another child I wanted to find because your story about her death bothered me."

She stood, her eyes pleading for him to understand. "I saw how much her loss haunted you. Now you can be free. Can't that be enough for now? She needs you," she said motioning to Lauren. "Rosaline is family. *My* family. I can take care of her."

It was a cruel choice, even though he knew Evelyn didn't mean to be. She couldn't know how much Rosaline had come to mean to him in such a short time.

Damian glanced at the fruit basket again, thought of the missing orange. He also noticed something else was missing.

What was Evelyn not telling him? How had Rosaline gotten the bracelet?

But now wasn't the time to argue. He sighed, resigned.

"Okay. I'll leave with Lauren."

Evelyn nodded relieved. "Good." She gave him information for a neighboring island where they were to meet. "Contact me when you've landed."

He nodded then escorted her to the door.

She grabbed his hand, searched his eyes. "I'm sorry you felt forced to come back here." She cupped the side of his face. "It wasn't supposed to happen this way. I'd never—"

"It's okay," he interrupted sensing her guilt as well as her love for him. "I'm glad I did. I needed to." It was hard to say, but it wasn't a lie.

He saw the shadow of a smile before Evelyn said, "Please trust me. I didn't mean to keep secrets I didn't want to get your hopes up about anything. I wanted to protect you."

He nodded, hearing the sincerity of her words.

"You know who sent Rosaline the bracelet and recording, don't you?"

She patted him on the chest and said in a curt tone, "Take care of your sister. Don't make a decision you'll regret." She turned and headed down the hall.

He watched her disappear around a corner then softly closed the door.

He turned to Lauren. "This is what we're going to do. I have a contact you're going to meet. You'll do exactly what he tells you."

Lauren looked at him both alarmed and confused. "But didn't Evelyn say—?"

He flashed a cold smile, his eyes turning to stone. "I said I wasn't leaving without Rosaline and I meant it."

30

Damian softened his tone seeing the unease in Lauren's gaze. "I don't know what's going on but I plan to find out. First, I need you to be safe and far away from here."

"But I—"

He grabbed her arms and held her gaze. "Listen to me. This is what I do. I help people and—"

"I know Damian, but—"

He turned from her. "This isn't a discussion."

Lauren made a noise of frustration. "Won't you just—"

"I can't think clearly if I'm worried about you. And—" He stopped when something hard hit the back of his head. He glanced down and saw an apple. He spun around and stared at her stunned. "Did you just throw that at me?"

"Yes, because I need you to listen. No," she held up her hand when he opened his mouth to argue, "shut up and listen. I mean it. I think I can help you."

It was unfair to laugh but he couldn't help himself. He

couldn't imagine this meek, fragile looking woman offering him much assistance.

"I appreciate the offer—"

"Let me help you! Even as children you never let me help you. Don't think that I'm that weak little girl I used to be. At five years old I learned the pain of blisters and the relief of calluses." Her voice shook, but she steadied it. "Don't look at me now and think you know who I am and what I'm capable of. You have no idea what my life has been like. But I can see this Rosaline means a lot to you. I can help you find her. We can rescue her together."

Damian fell silent surprised by the ferocity of her tone, amazed by the courage of the woman who dared to talk back to him. He also felt the bitterness of shame. He hadn't meant to disregard her hardship; to belittle the child who'd been forced to work like a slave before she'd found her way into a wealthy family. He had to fight not to be angry on her behalf. To rail against the unfairness of it all. The years stolen from them. But now wasn't the time. He wouldn't risk losing her again.

He may not know the woman his little sister had become, but he would respect her.

Humbled, Damian slowly nodded for Lauren to continue and began to sit, ready to listen.

"I think Rosaline might still be here."

He paused halfway between sitting and standing. "Excuse me?"

"I think Rosaline might still be here," Lauren repeated.

Damian straightened and stared at her stunned. "How?"

"When you were talking to Evelyn I thought I heard something."

"Like what?"

"Moaning."

"Where?"

"I don't know." She pressed a finger to her lips. "That's why I need you to be quiet."

He fell silent and waited.

Lauren softly walked around the room then paused when she reached the front entrance. She stopped then pointed to the closet.

Damian cautiously approached then swung the door open.

At first he didn't see anything inside the closet's deep interior until he turned on the light and saw high heels shoes on their side, which wouldn't have meant much to him if they hadn't been attached to feet.

His incredulous gaze swept up to legs and a black, sheath dress, a velvet choker on a long neck supporting a head that had slumped forward like a broken mannequin.

He rushed forward and bent over the figure, gently tilted her head back, half hoping that the face revealed to him didn't belong to Rosaline.

But...then...oh please no...an almost bloodless replica of the woman he loved faced him, her eyes closed, her skin cold when he touched her neck.

He couldn't find a pulse. But there had to be one.

Damian fell to his knees, placing his hands on the ground on either side of her to keep from grabbing her. He wouldn't panic even though for some reason his palms suddenly felt wet and sticky when he gripped them together.

He took a deep breath, checked for a pulse again, released a sigh. It was faint but it was there. He drew his hand back surprised to see a red smudge on her neck that hadn't been there before.

He absently wiped his hands on the front of his shirt, annoyed by how sweaty they felt. It wasn't like him to sweat so much.

He glanced down at his hands and paused at the sight of his palms—stained red.

Blood red.

Blood? How could there be blood?

His gaze swept the closet falling on the tiny puddle next to Rosaline's body before landing on the knife protruding out of her side. The position of her knees had initially hid it from view.

How could this have happened? Why? Rage coursed through him. What was Evelyn hiding now? Was this why someone had wanted Rosaline to come here?

He heard Lauren gasp, which got his spinning mind back into focus.

Lauren pressed her hands together. "Is she...?"

"Yes," Damian said but before he could say more Rosaline's eyes fluttered open. "You've got my blood on you," she said, sounding almost satisfied as if solving a mystery. "So that's what it meant."

She wasn't making sense. Was she delirious? Didn't matter. At least she was alive.

"Rosaline," Damian said. "We're going to get you some help. Stay awake for me. Who attacked you?"

"Did you find her?"

For a moment Damian's mind went blank then he realized she meant Evelyn.

"Yes. I did."

"Good."

"Yes, she's breathing and conscious," he heard Lauren tell the dispatcher.

"Tell me who attacked you."

Rosaline swallowed and drew her brows together in pain. "I made a mistake. I frightened him."

"No," Lauren said, starting to sound frustrated, "we don't know what happened yet, we just need medical care."

"Who?" Damian asked, trying to focus on Rosaline and not his desire to snatch the phone from Lauren and speak to the dispatcher himself.

"The boy."

Damian blinked surprised.

The boy had done this to her? The boy he'd brought back to the hotel room? He hadn't read him right? Had the boy tried to rob her? Damian inwardly cursed himself for putting Rosaline in harm's way.

"No, we don't need the police," Lauren said. "We need an ambulance."

"The boy?" Damian repeated just to make sure.

"Yes."

He felt ill. "Rosaline I—"

"Don't apologize," she said with a tired shake of her head. "I was trying to help him and told him things about himself I shouldn't have. He got scared and thought I was a witch. When I tried to calm him down he...grabbed the knife. He only wanted to escape. He didn't mean it. He shoved me in here and I hit my head hard, I must have passed out. I don't remember much." She glanced behind him to stare at Lauren who was still on the phone talking to the dispatcher.

"Who is she? She moves like you. Especially when you're upset."

Damian brushed her cheek, wishing it didn't feel so cold, not ready to reveal the truth. He didn't want her to think of anything else. She needed to reserve what little strength she had left. He didn't want to think of how long she'd been like this. "I'll tell you later."

"When?"

When you're out of the hospital and safely off this island, he wanted to tell her but instead kissed her forehead and said, "When you're better."

Moments later the response team arrived.

Before Damian raced with the EMTs down the hall Damian turned to Lauren and said, "Tell Evelyn we found Rosaline and then you're both going to tell me what the hell is going on."

EVELYN HEARD the child before she spotted him. A trembling, sniveling figure hidden in the stairwell. He looked up at her and gasped.

She recognized Marcel, a bright boy who'd been sold when his desperate family needed money. She'd found him to be a helpful child when she'd spoken to him at different times.

"What's wrong?" she asked him.

He wiped his eyes. "I met a witch. She had dark skin and a deep voice." He jumped to his feet. "And I stabbed her," he mimed the action as if thrusting a knife into someone." His face and hands fell. "But now..." He shook his head. "I am sorry. So sorry."

"Are you afraid she cursed you?"

He shook his head. "She was nice," he said in a choked voice. "But her words—"

"They scared you?"

He nodded.

"What did she say?"

He paused before he said, "My life would soon end. That another I'd get."

Evelyn sighed. She'd wondered if Marcel could have been the boy Damian had referenced and his description of 'the witch' could have been Rosaline. But her words sounded very similar to one of Rosaline's cryptic flashes. No wonder the boy was frightened.

But Evelyn was frightened to...worried about the fate of her granddaughter. She kept her voice calm when she said, "Where is she now?"

"In the closet."

She had to tell Damian. They had to make sure Rosaline was okay. "Wait here," she told Marcel then turned to go back to the hotel suite. She stopped when her cell phone alerted her to a text from Lauren. *We found her. Calling an ambulance.*

Evelyn briefly closed her eyes in relief. Rosaline was okay. Marcel hadn't killed her.

But Rosaline's words to him let Evelyn know what she had to do. The boy's life as he knew it would end tonight. No one had come to collect him yet. It would take some planning, but she'd manage it. She would help him disappear.

Evelyn held out her hand to Marcel, briefly remembering a little boy she'd rescued over twenty-some years ago who'd changed her life forever. One whose beautiful, but sad brown eyes hadn't changed. She hoped meeting his sister again would finally relieve him of his ghosts. That it would be the key to unlocking his guarded heart.

But now for now she couldn't think about Damian.

Here she had another chance to make a change.

With fear, hope and trust another little boy cautiously took her hand, eager for the promise of freedom.

31

An empress entered the hospital waiting room.

Gone was the shuffling gait, the worn clothes. Evelyn sat down next to Damian in one of the uniform chairs lining the perimeter of the room as if sitting on a throne.

She stared straight ahead, didn't utter a word. Next to him Damian could feel Lauren's uncertain gaze. She opened her mouth to speak, but Damian raised his hands to stop her.

Hours had passed since Rosaline's arrival at the hospital. Large windows welcomed the hazy pink gaze of a rising sun as if gently nudging the city awake.

But the hospital buzzed with the never resting energy of an ant colony. The state of art hospital belied the provinciality of the island. The scent of money touched every aspect of the building from the gleaming reception desk and flat screen monitors, the comfortable seats in the waiting area, to the steel elevators and multi-national hospital staff. He knew Rosaline was in capable hands, but it did little to ease his anger.

Damian leaned forward, resting his elbows on his lap and said in a soft voice, "I'm waiting."

"I heard she'll make a full recovery," Evelyn said. "That they're waiting to take her to another room."

He shook his head tired and weary. He wasn't in the mood for idle chit chat. He wanted answers. "No more games, Evelyn."

She slowly stood. "Walk with me."

Moments later they stood outside near one of the many benches in front of the hospital, Evelyn shivered against the morning breeze that brushed passed with a slight chill. Damian took off his dinner jacket and held it out to her, but she shook her head and said something that was drowned out by the wail of an ambulance roaring past.

"Just take it," he said, not caring about her reason.

"No." She glanced at his shirt with a pointed look of regret. "It's hard to look at you."

He followed her gaze then remembered his blood stained shirt. He swore and put on his jacket and buttoned the front. "Better?"

Evelyn looked up at the sky, the early morning still holding onto some darkness, casting shadows along the trees and shrubbery.

"I didn't plan it to happen this way." After a pause she said, "Years ago, I came to this island to fulfill my dream of working in the movies." She nodded at his look of surprise. "Yes, just like your mother except I did it a different way. I knew it was a long shot, but I still dreamed big." She laughed without humor. "I always thought I was born too late. In the early days of film, women used to dominate the movie business. Before 1925 half of all scripts were written by woman.

"Unfortunately, that ended when men discovered there

was money to be made and kicked most of the powerful females out of the producer, director, scriptwriter positions. But that didn't stop me from dreaming of making movies. I initially tried the traditional route but the movies at the time only wanted a certain type of black experience and I didn't fit the mold. I even tried smaller films on my own. I admit they were terrible.

"I didn't have the right connections or money to get my vision out there even in the nineties and the introduction of digital film. Until, at a New York party of a mutual friend, I met a statuesque beauty with ebony skin and luminous, intricately braided jet black hair dressed in a desert green dress and large hoop earrings. She was a talented, brilliant actress who'd had minor success in the mainstream industry but felt stifled and was determined to make indie pictures. She had connections and money and I had the ideas. We became partners and eventually used a local man as a figurehead because that's how you got respect in those days. Besides, he owned a club and that was one way to scout talent."

Damian shook his head. "What does this have to do...?"

"I'm getting there. Be patient." Evelyn started walking the length of the building.

He sighed and followed her.

"I wrote scripts and worked as a stuntwoman. She scouted the locations and was the one who decided that we could shoot most of our films here. It was cheap. So cheap we made a lot of movies on this island. Plus, the government was easy to work with, eager to welcome any activity that was lucrative." She sent him a quick glance then let her gaze fall to the ground. "At least that's what I was made to believe."

Evelyn shook her head with a heavy sigh. "I truly thought I was just filming movies. Flashy, campy and, sometimes, satirical movies. I left the distribution and money to her. I was having too much fun to care. To really pay attention. If I had, I would have started to wonder sooner how our tiny direct-to-video films, mostly marketed on the internet, could be making such a profit. They weren't the greatest, but good fun. At the time, I thought we were fulfilling a need. I never thought there was more to it until one night I was in the office and overheard her taking to someone about the costume division and how lucrative it was. That made no sense to me. Why would this division, that I'd never heard of, be profitable?"

"I soon discovered what was really going on. That she and the club owner were exploiting children and running an underground business in the sex trade. I learned that one of our 'investors' targeted single mothers, promising them a chance to be in one of our pictures." Evelyn nodded at Damian's surprise. "Yes, what happened to you wasn't a mistake. Your cousin and mother were both used by this man because you and your sister were profitable to him.

"Once I found out, I made it my mission to dismantle this business enterprise but realized it was a lot bigger than I was. There were too many political figures with power and sway involved so I decided to steal 'the merchandise.'

"And this might sound ridiculous but my granddaughter told me how. She'd drawn a picture of me flying through the air, I thought she'd somehow seen one of our movies, but then it gave me an idea and the beginning of a new business began.

"Without Rosaline I may not have been there that night to get you. She told me about one of her flashes. About a boy with angry, sad eyes. By taking you that day, I found a new purpose. With the help of a clever businessman from a neighboring island, referred to me by a computer graphic designer I'd been dating, I was able to come back often and became a thorn in their side until I brought the business to its knees. They were forced to go even deeper underground a mere shadow of what they used to be. My former partner never forgave me."

"Why didn't you ever tell me about her or Rosaline?"

Evelyn laughed. "Would you really have believed my life's work started with the vision and drawing of a kindergartner?"

Damian shook his head. "No."

"And I never wanted you to know that I was even remotely connected to the organization responsible for what had happened to you. I forced your father to keep it a secret."

Damian shook his head, amused. "Let me guess, Dad was the 'clever businessman'?"

Evelyn nodded. "To this day, people don't know. We kept our connection secret, just in case anyone came after one of us. I don't know if you remember how long it took for you to finally meet him."

"A year, wasn't it?"

"About. We didn't want to do anything hasty. We made things as convoluted as possible in case anyone was paying attention. When we thought things were safe, he adopted you while he also helped me come up with a system to handle other rescues, although he never got personally involved.

"Just like I kept my involvement with your father secret, I wanted to protect Rosaline and it wasn't something I thought you needed to know. Her gift isn't always a good thing. I nearly lost her once when someone tried to kidnap her thinking she was a seer who they could profit from. Plus,

Rosaline doesn't like anyone to know what she can do because it's not something she can control."

Damian hesitated then said, "Did she know about Lauren?"

"No." Evelyn sighed. She turned and headed back towards the benches. "But she did know about the bracelet. I don't know why she showed you. She has her own strange reasons. Perhaps she wanted to see how you'd respond because I never told her specifically about you."

"But you talk often about other things?"

She frowned. "Talk? With Rosaline? I rarely talk to her on the phone. We have other ways of communicating."

Damian nodded, tucking that information away, not ready to unpack it because it only led to more questions.

"My team and I haven't stopped working on this island," Evelyn continued. "Some of the rescues have been close calls.

"You weren't supposed to notice I was missing. I thought things with Lauren would take a couple of days but we had some issues with the funds transfer." She waved his question away. "I'll get to that now.

"I found out about Lauren by accident three years ago, in connection to my former partner. I had no idea who Lauren Metcliff really was. That's why I didn't tell you about her.

"I started dating a man who told me about his niece. That he'd always been suspicious of how his brother had adopted her. He told me he feared for her and asked me to look into it and then I got suspicious too. They had both been working with their father's business when the brother 'adopted' a young girl on this very island.

"I wouldn't be surprised if my former partner had told

Everett Metcliff or someone else about the cabin I'd bought years ago. She'd helped me get it. Anyway, Lauren's uncle had convinced her to help him take Everett down. Lauren had felt more and more under his thumb, even after the marriage he'd arranged for her, not knowing that his brother had been a few steps ahead of him choosing someone Lauren could trust.

"So then we came up with a plan. With her husband's help, she'd disappear with the important shares Everett needed and some other assets he'd put under her name.

"He'd sent the hunters to scare me into telling him her whereabouts, but his brother had his own team dispose of them."

Damian frowned. "But that doesn't explain who sent the clues to Rosaline."

"Shapiro wasn't wrong. There was a third party, but not how we initially thought. I think my former partner tried to lure Rosaline to enact her revenge. Recently, one of our rescues was an expensive exchange that I stopped and that likely enraged her. The voice recording and the vines were her signature. She's good at mimicry. But she underestimated something."

"What?"

"Your father's love for you."

Damian's voice cracked in surprise. "My father?"

"Have you met his latest girlfriend yet?"

"No, and Lucas even mentioned that it was strange."

"It is strange to meet the woman you've been keeping track of for years. One you've seen in the movies many times."

His brows shot up. "Don't tell me Rilina the Elephant Queen?"

Evelyn nodded. "That's her. The lead actress, although I did most of the stunts."

"He can't be seeing her," Damian said alarmed. "If she's as dangerous as you've said—"

"Damian—"

"He needs to be warned." He pulled out his cell phone. "I have to get a hold of Lucas and have him check in on Dad. I didn't get a chance to speak to him. She picked up the phone." He swore. "Damn, I shouldn't have let that pass."

Evelyn took the phone from him. "Your father's safe. Ian made sure."

"Ian?"

"Yes, he said Rosaline told him to."

"Rosaline? But how?"

"You'd have to ask them. All I know is that by trying to get to me she was also putting you in danger so your father played the innocent while he coaxed her to tell him about her plans for revenge. She's always been eager to tell others about how she's been wronged, never could keep her mouth shut. However, I hadn't realized how close she'd gotten to me until recently when you and Rosaline both showed up here. Your father was keeping his own secrets."

Damian headed to the hospital entrance. "Then Rosaline's still not safe—"

Evelyn grabbed his arm and stopped him. "She won't bother us anymore."

He folded his arms. "Did my dad stop her?"

She shrugged. "We both did, in a manner of speaking. Right now she's on her way to a foreign country to attend an awards ceremony held in her honor, that doesn't exist, where she'll inconveniently lose her papers and passport. He's been preparing the scheme for a while now so she won't suspect a thing when she arrives and realizes she can never leave."

He nodded impressed. "So what happens now?"

"Lauren's disappearance was also a distraction so that Everett didn't look into what is really happening with his ironworks company. However, the subterfuge is now complete so she can return to the States. She had enough time to transfer funds to Metcliff's brother and now she doesn't have to worry. He'll take care of the rest."

"But Everett could still..." Damian's words fell away as Evelyn shook her head.

"No, Everett may be able to survive the loss of his business, properties and assets but his reputation is his pride and joy and with one stroke his brother could expose what's in the Metcliff closet and completely destroy him."

BERMUDA

Patton Metcliff looked at the share transfer on his cell phone with grim satisfaction before he set it down on his desk. A sweet island breeze filtered through the open door of his study carrying the scent of nutmeg.

He leaned back in his chair and glanced at the silver framed picture facing him.

The picture of a happy little dachshund name Lucy. The sweetest dog a child could have.

He never believed she ran away. She loved him too much. He remembered the warm weight of her when she'd snuggle up with him in bed, the soft feel of her brown fur that soothed him when he got anxious.

She'd been brave and loyal.

Despite her small size she'd saved him many times.

When his brother tried to hold him under the water when they were playing at the lake house, her insistent barking had alerted others.

When his brother pretended to 'accidentally' kick him with a soccer ball she'd growled at him.

Lucy had comforted Patton from the bullying his parents chose to ignore. They thought that he needed to be toughed up and that his older brother, Everett, was the key. Better to be bullied by your brother than some stranger, his father used to tell him. He'll force you to be strong. It's a cruel world. He's a good teacher. One day you'll thank him.

Patton drummed his fingers on the desk.

His brother taught him many things: The biggest being that he couldn't open his mouth without lying.

He'd lied to the world about adopting a little girl.

He'd lied to his emotionally fragile second wife that the child was really the result of an affair, just so that he could prove their fertility issues were her fault instead of his. (That's when Patton had grown suspicious. He knew his brother was too careful with his seed to get a woman pregnant unless it served his purposes and he'd never want a woman to have power over him).

He'd lied to the little girl that he cared about her while constantly belittling her and reminding her that she'd been bought and paid and that she'd end up in the gutter again without him.

His brother always thought that he was the smartest person in the room.

Patton grinned. He enjoyed letting him believe that. What his brother hadn't taught him, what Patton had learned on his own, was patience.

Lucy would get her revenge.

Patton would watch his brother lose everything.

And he'd laugh.

33

—————

"Close your eyes."

Those weren't the first words Rosaline had expected Damian to say when he finally came to see her. He stood just outside the door of the private hospital room he'd managed to get her.

"Are they closed?"

She was eager to see him, it was a difficult request, but she obeyed. "Yes."

She heard him walk into the room, felt him stand near the bed.

She smiled, wondering what kind of surprise he might have in store for her. "Can I open them now?"

She felt him take her hand in his before he said in a quiet voice, "No."

"I can't wait to get out of here. We're flying out tomorrow, right?"

He tenderly stroked the back of her hand. "Hmm."

She frowned, he was uncustomarily subdued. From Evelyn, she'd learned about his reunion with his sister and had expected him to be happy, but his mood was anything but. "Damian? What's wrong?"

He released her hand. "You lied to me."

Rosaline's eyes flew open, she stared at him startled, seeing the sad shades of blue and black reflecting in his aura before he swiftly covered her eyes with his hand. "Don't look at me."

She tried to remove his hand. "What is going on? Lied? I've never lied to you."

"You hadn't tried to call Evelyn, she told me so. You knew about the bracelet. You knew about the little boy Evelyn had rescued and you pretended not to."

"I didn't know specifics—"

"You didn't need to. You're smart enough to put pieces together. That's why you knew there was more to my story than I'd initially told you. I'd thought it was because of your gift, but it was because you were hiding things from me. You knew when Evelyn found me, it wasn't my first time. That I did know what I was there for, that the apartment was owned by the people I worked for."

He took a deep breath. "You kept asking for my trust, you listened as I bared my soul to you, but you didn't do the same." He let his hand fall. "You kept telling me I wasn't asking the right questions. I should have known then. I should have asked why your ring was on Evelyn's bedroom dresser. I should have asked if you'd moved the chair. I should have asked you about the map hidden on the side of the cabin. But I didn't, so you strung me along—"

Rosaline opened her eyes but kept her gaze lowered. "That's not true."

"Then tell me what's true." Damian stepped back and opened his arms wide. "You see everything. I can't...I can't hide anything from you. I'm constantly at your mercy. You know me better than I know myself. So what do you see now, hmm?"

Rosaline swallowed, her mouth suddenly dry. She still didn't have the courage to look at him. To face his anger and disappointment. She hadn't realized how much she'd kept from him, how much he'd resent her for it. "I took off my ring when I was tidying up, it didn't seem important. I didn't tell you about the bracelet because I wasn't sure."

"But you saw my reaction to it," Damian challenged. "So you knew what it meant, you knew who I was."

"Yes, but I... I really wanted to hear your story from you. I promise you that Evelyn didn't tell me your name or what had happened after the rescue, she only told me what the bracelets meant. And when I saw the one for Lauren I didn't want to make any assumptions. I didn't want to give you false hope." She sighed, rubbed her eyes. "And you're right. I should have told you my connection to the island, but it seemed so fantastical about a flash I had as a young child, I didn't want to sully your memory of how you'd met Evelyn. I wanted you to believe it was fate."

"Just like you wanted to believe it was fate that brought us both to the cabin?"

"It was fate."

"Really? Why did you lie about calling her?"

Rosaline hesitated. "I thought you'd find it strange that I'd known she hadn't been at the cabin because I'd moved her chair. I'd been there a week before and it had felt different so I shifted the chair to see what she would do. She'd usually shift it back. It was a signal we came up with. When I came back at the same time you did and saw the chair hadn't been moved I knew something was wrong."

"And you couldn't tell me that?"

She cautiously looked up at him. "I didn't think to."

Damian released a sigh of frustration. "Of course you didn't. You liked remaining a mystery. That's your power, that's how you manipulate people."

Rosaline shook her head. "No, that's really not—"

"Doesn't matter." He rested his hands on his hips. "Amazing how chatty you can be when it suits you."

"I don't usually—"

"It's best we end things now."

"Damian please," Rosaline said, her heart constricting with the pain of rejection. "I'm sorry. I didn't mean..." She closed her eyes and held back tears feeling like a fool. She'd had a chance to gain the trust of this wonderful man and she'd ruined it because she'd been too busy protecting herself and what others perceived as her oddities. She didn't know what to do. How to fix it.

"Didn't mean what?" He pressed her to finish. "You didn't mean for me to find out?"

"I didn't mean to hurt you."

"Oh." He sniffed in derision. "Is that what my aura's telling you? That I'm hurt?"

She knew it was pain that forced him to mock her, but his criticism still stung.

She boldly stared at him and he boldly held her gaze, forcing her to see the searing red that surrounded him. The rage surprised her. She softened her voice and reached for him. "Damian, I'm so—"

He drew away from her. "Don't try to comfort me." He turned from her and stared out the window. "I don't need it because I'm not hurt. I'm ashamed." He fell silent a moment before he said in a low voice, "You know the worst thing about all this? All that's happened? I realized I'm nobody's hero. I didn't find you, Lauren did. I didn't find Evelyn, she found me. I've fooled myself all these years that I mattered. But it's been a lie. I didn't protect my sister, I didn't protect you. Evelyn didn't need me. Ian made sure our dad was okay," he paused, flashed a sour grin, "thanks to you." He took a deep breath. "The truth is when I look at you I'm ashamed of myself. That I'd been tricked and then blackmailed into a life I've had to hide all these years. That a reckless choice I made nearly got you killed.

"I'm embarrassed that it was a little girl who rescued me because I couldn't save myself. And that's who you see when you look at me. You don't depend on me, you depend on yourself and I don't blame you."

Rosaline stared at him. She didn't know what to say, she wasn't good with revealing what was in her heart. She didn't know how to convey how valuable and wonderful he was to her. That she didn't need a hero. That he was enough.

But he read her silence as confirmation and she saw his shoulders fall. She shook her head. "No, it's not what you think. I-I don't know what to say." She waved her hands helpless. "It's not that I don't have anything to say." She let her hands fall to her lap. "Please give me another chance. I can change."

Damian shook his head. "I'd never ask you to change. Especially for me." He took her hands in his, his grip gentle and warm. "Thanks for saving my life. One day I'll repay my debt to you."

Rosaline's heart pounded with panic and fear. That's not what she wanted. He didn't have to repay anything. How could she make him understand? What had Evelyn told him?

But her mouth wouldn't move and the chasm between them grew bigger.

And bigger.

Until there was only the sound of unhurried, receding footsteps, the soft closing of a door and the salty taste of her tears.

34

It was better this way.

Brendan, Sandra and Aidan were fine.

His father was fine.

His brothers were fine.

His sister was fine.

Evelyn was fine.

Rosaline was safe.

Everything was back as it should be. He had no one close who he had to worry about. No one close whose life depended on him. He'd continue to rescue strangers.

Damian returned to the waiting room with a steely resolve, wondering if he'd been able to hide how shaken he'd been. That his failure to protect her was one of the key reasons he couldn't see her gain.

It was true that he was no hero. That he'd failed her. While he was in the club drinking and talking to his mother, reuniting with Evelyn in the hotel basement, meeting his sister again in the hallway then the hotel suite, all that time Rosalina had been left languishing in a closet. He struggled to stop the image of her prone body with a protruding knife from repeating in his mind.

Yes, he was angry about all she'd hidden from him. He could forgive her that. But he couldn't forgive himself. The reality that he'd never be the kind of man she'd fully turn to.

The waiting room had gotten busier when he finally reached it. Lauren rose to her feet when she saw him.

He tucked his pain away and smiled at her. At least he had his sister. She was enough for him. She wouldn't keep secrets. She would fully trust him.

"She's doing well," he told her, then before she could ask him anything else, he said what had been burning in his mind since he'd first discovered who she was.

"You could have hidden out anywhere. Why did you come back here?"

"Because I wanted to see the school."

"School? What school?"

A secretive smile touched her lips. "Come on. Let me show you."

FAR OUTSIDE OF THE CITY, past the pristine suburban homes, past the boarded up houses, dilapidated shacks, abandoned cars and empty lots, nestled at the base of a mountain with a view of the ocean, sat a spacious orange and brown compound that had once been the monument to a woman's ambition and greed but now echoed with the voices and laughter of children.

Children, aged five to fourteen, proudly dressed in white and dark blue uniforms seemed to be everywhere as the school day came to a close. They flooded out the entrance in pairs and groups, some jumping on bicycles, others looped arm-in-arm as they headed home. A sea of them made their way along the corridors of the two-story building its numerous windows filling the building with natural light.

With pride, the headmistress showed Lauren and Damian the library, kitchen, playground, seven classrooms (built for play and exploration), courtyard and latrines.

It was a place where the children could feel safe and learn.

When her former partner had been forced to abandon her vanity project and take her organization further underground, Evelyn had taken over the building. It also included dormitories where half the students (those rescued from the streets and gangs, with no home to return to; others whose parents couldn't afford them) lived.

The building not only changed the lives of the children but also the adults who worked as teachers, cooks, groundskeepers, and electricians and could gain new skills to improve their lives and have other options to support their families.

Days earlier Lauren had come to see the school with Evelyn and had been amazed by its transformation, but she'd studied it with the cool distance of Lauren Metcliff.

Now, standing outside the building as a soft breeze swept over the green grass, ruffled the leaves of the palm trees and swept up by the sweet, floral scent of the golden yellow, trumpet shaped allamanda plant as it crawled along the ground, she saw it as Carin Bouchard.

She felt the sun on her back and briefly remembered carrying the bricks, the blisters. Lauren didn't realize she was shaking until she felt Damian's comforting arm, resting on her shoulders.

There were many things she didn't remember about him. She'd forgotten how dark his lashes were, the softness of his skin, she hadn't imagined he'd grow up to be so handsome, but she'd never forgotten how safe he always made her feel. How kind he was.

A sob of joy and sorrow escaped her. She turned to him and wrapped her arms around him with an almost jealous possession. There was no Evelyn, no Rosaline to compete with. At that moment he belonged solely to her again.

"This is the school I'd wanted for you," she said into his shirt. "For us. I missed you so much. I never imagined this day would come. That we'd ever be together again."

He didn't respond but he held her just as tightly as if he were afraid to lose her again.

After a few minutes she drew away and wiped her eyes. "Tell me the story of Hansel and Gretel."

He blinked surprised.

"Evelyn told me it was your favorite story." When he ducked his head embarrassed she took his hand. "I know so little about you. I want to know what you enjoy. Please, tell me the story."

"I'm sure you already know it," he said in a gruff voice.

She squeezed his hand. "I still want to hear it from you."

So, as they walked along the perimeters of the building a man who'd learned to hope again told his beloved sister a fairy tale.

A story about children surviving when the adults in their lives were the last people they could depend on. But they could depend on each other.

At the end of his tale they walked back to the rented car.

"I'm so glad I got to see this again with you," Lauren said and her heart lifted when she saw her brother's smile, it wasn't forced and it was truly beautiful when he said, "Me too," but his eyes, his beautiful eyes were still sad.

And she wondered if his sadness had anything to do with Rosaline but was too afraid to ask.

Even when they left the island together, without Rosaline, something he'd vowed he wouldn't do.

35

$\mathcal{A}$ cold February wind stung Rosaline's face as her boots crunched over frosted leaves, a canopy of snow dusted trees intermittently scattering snowflakes, which reminded her of sugar crystals, as they fell gently onto her red wool coat. The basket felt heavy in her hand as she walked towards her grandmother's cabin, the afternoon walk from the main road where a taxi had dropped her, feeling longer than usual.

It had been two months since she'd returned from Carliz.

Two months since she'd gotten her heart broken.

She hadn't planned on returning to the cabin until the following autumn, her memories of Damian still too fresh in her mind, but her mother had insisted that Rosaline check on her grandmother who was getting over a cold. No amount of pleading would convince her mother to go instead. "Isn't it enough that I work two shifts?" her mother chided her over the phone. "You haven't even come by and seen me in weeks."

"I've been busy," Rosaline said, which wasn't a complete

lie. She'd made sure to focus more on growing her business, accepting more clients than she had in the past.

"Plus you can schedule your own hours and you're better with the sick than I am."

Rosaline stared out at the expansive space outside her kitchen window for the first time feeling alone. "Mom, you're a nurse."

"It's different with family," she said in a tart voice. "What's wrong with you? You love helping people. You've never complained before."

She'd never had a reason to. She'd never dreaded that her grandmother's cabin would become a shrine to all that she'd lost.

But she knew she had to get over her pain. The cabin had once been a special place for her and she would reclaim it again.

Rosaline stopped in front of the cabin door and knocked.

When no one replied she used her key and entered, surprised by the scent of cinnamon rolls, the warmth coming from a crackling fire. Someone was definitely here. She closed the door and called out, "Nan?"

She paused when she saw large boots, then looked and saw a large jacket.

A familiar jacket.

Her first instinct was to run. If Damian was there he wouldn't want to see her. Perhaps he'd come to check on Evelyn too.

She remembered his anger, his hurt, his disappointment. She couldn't face him again.

She turned to escape.

"It's all right," a deep voice said, floating towards her from the back of the cabin. "Come, Rosaline."

She swallowed, carefully set the basket on the table then crept towards the bedroom. She lowered her senses; she knew how much he hated her ability to read his aura. She would only read his body language and listen to his words. Nothing else.

She gently widened the partially opened door where she saw a man sitting on the side of her grandmother's bed.

"I wasn't sure you'd come," Damian said. "Evelyn said you would."

"I wasn't expecting you."

"I know."

Rosaline searched his face. He didn't look angry, he didn't look sad. He almost looked relieved to see her.

Was this a dream?

He motioned her forward then he patted the space beside him.

She shook her head.

His mouth curved into a smile.

"It's okay," he said. "I'm not mad anymore." He stood. "Yes, I was mad then," he said reading the question in her eyes. "It still hurts all that you kept from me." He held up his hand, waving her words away. "No need to defend yourself. I understand now. You didn't want to lose me. You were afraid you'd scare me off." He walked towards her, causing Rosaline's heart to flutter with each step. "And you were right. I was scared. I was scared of you. How much you could see of me.

"But that's when I realized your true gift. That you could see a flawed man like me and still want him. Still...care for him. Forgive me for not seeing it sooner."

Rosaline lowered her eyes, gripped her hands, determined not to read his aura, desperate to take him at his words. "I'm sorry too," she said, although her words felt inadequate. "I didn't mean to—"

"I didn't come here to hear your apology." He stopped in front of her and lifted her chin. "Look at me. No, don't close your eyes. I mean it. Please look at me."

She released a long breath then met his eyes but didn't look past the urgent plea that reflected in his brown gaze.

"I thought I could forget you. I thought finding Evelyn and meeting Carin again would be enough. But I was wrong." His gaze dipped to her throat. "I've become a greedy man, Rosaline." He lowered his head and kissed her neck, his breath hot on her skin when he said, "I want more." His smoldering gaze met and held hers. "So much more." He unbuttoned her coat. "I'm hungry." He pushed her coat from her shoulders until it fell to the ground. "Very, very hungry."

What Damian didn't tell her was how his brothers had reminded him of that hunger. How he'd been forced to ignore Lucas' calls, how he'd read through his stack of romance novels and had bought five more, trying to prove to himself that he was okay, but never being able to touch the novel he'd promised to read with her.

He spent as much time as he could with his sister. He hadn't met her husband Casey yet because she said their relationship was 'complicated.'

He visited Brendan and his family.

He fixed his father's porch step.

He welcomed the New Year alone ignoring his brother Lucas's pleas to attend his party.

He felt the ache of emptiness, no longer taking comfort in the space that had once felt as close to home as he could make it.

He would have continued to delude himself that he was

fine if he hadn't walked into his apartment one afternoon and been greeted by the scent of lavender and eucalyptus.

Scents that reminded him of Rosaline. His heart began to race. Why would his apartment smell like her?

The tinny sound of a cell phone pierced the air with a news announcement.

...CEO Everett Metcliff dies in fiery single-car collision.

Damian tentatively closed the door and followed the sound.

...The distraught father had only recently reunited with his missing daughter.

He saw his brother sitting on the mustard colored sofa, gazing down at his cell phone.

Damian buried the sting of disappointment. There was no Rosaline. Had he suffered an olfactory hallucination? Was he missing her that much?

He tucked the questions away and sat down beside his brother and began to ask him, "What do you want?" until he realized the scent was even stronger. "Why do you smell like Rosaline?" he asked him.

Ian continued to stare at his cell phone as another news story hit his screen.

...Can enjoy the hot new restaurant that serves a seven course meal...for your pet.

He pulled a note out of his jeans' pocket. He rested it on the coffee table.

Damian picked up the note and instantly recognized Rosaline's handwriting.

It was instructions for a special cream she'd made for Ian.

Damian read the note twice, a burning jealousy threatened to consume him. All these months they'd kept in touch. Without him.

As children, while his brother Lucas was checking for monsters under the bed and closet, Ian had watched him.

A constant observer, he never made Damian feel uneasy. He had a comforting, guarding air about him. Although Lucas acted like the eldest, Ian truly was.

He'd been quiet back then, even more so. Damian would catch Ian watching him across the dining room table, on the playground, in the school lunchroom. He could always feel his brother's probing gaze.

Ian only watched Damian when he sensed something was wrong.

Their father had once joked that Damian would starve at a buffet because he was known for taking the barest minimum amount of food, especially when he felt anxious, guilty or afraid. Damian never wanted to take more than he thought he deserved. But Ian would always find a way to give him food. He'd slip an extra slice of spiced bun on Damian's dinner plate or sneak a chocolate bar in Damian's backpack.

Ian studied his brother now, the cell phone silent as it sat on the couch cushion, causing the apartment to descend into an eerie quiet.

Ian sent a pointed look at the note then looked at Damian again.

Damian tossed the note on the table and began to pace. He paced liked a caged animal. A cage he'd put himself into.

"She betrayed me. She didn't tell me things. She knows too much about me."

Ian nodded.

"I've got all that I need. I don't need..." He caught his brother's frown. "Yes, all right. I admit it. I'm afraid. I'm afraid of asking too much. I'm afraid I'm not good enough. That I'll let her down. If you'd seen her in that closet..."

Ian stood, took Damian's hand and placed the note in it. He met his brother's gaze.

"Go on and say it," Damian pressed. "Say something. Tell me what a coward I am."

Ian closed Damian's fingers around the note. "Stop starving," he said in a quiet voice before he affectionately patted Damian's cheek, grabbed his cane and walked out.

Damian stared down at his fist. He had spent his life denying so much, afraid he wasn't worthy. But at that moment he stopped being afraid.

The hunger too deep to ignore.

So, days later, when he finally held the woman he'd been craving for so long, he kissed her without hunger but complete surrender. There was nothing more to fight.

And the divine pleasure she found in his kiss caused Rosaline to forget everything.

She forgot about the basket on the table.

She forgot about the shock of seeing his boots.

She forgot about being scared.

Instead, when Damian's bare skin touched hers, she felt the need to satiate her own hunger. To melt into the caress of his large hands, as they cascaded over her body, indulge in the hot, sensuous trail of his tongue, savor the waves of ecstasy when their bodies moved in exquisite harmony.

The world outside the cabin faded away until the fire died and the pink and orange hues of evening settled in the room.

Rosaline released a sigh of satisfaction, her body languid with pleasure, as they lay in each other's arms, neither ready to leave the bed yet. "What do you see when you look at me?" Damian asked her.

Rosaline knew he wanted to know what his aura told her, what emotions he revealed.

But she knew that's not what he needed. It was time to tell him something he didn't know. Something she'd never told him before. Something she'd known all those months ago when she'd first met him.

She held his gaze, playfully tracing the line of his jaw when saw a brief moment of uncertainty enter his eyes. She knew how vulnerable he felt. So instead of answering him right away Rosaline told him a story.

A story about a little house that longed for a mustard colored couch, a blue mosaic print lampshade, and a stack of romance novels.

Slowly, she saw the uncertainty in his gaze fade to joy, as he realized she was describing a space where his furniture would fit.

A place he could call home.

"What do I see?" she said.

"Yes,"Damian said the word, as heated as his gaze. "Tell me what you see."

Rosaline lightly kissed his lips and smiled before she whispered, "I see my future. I see the man I love."

ABOUT THE AUTHOR

Dara Girard, an award-winning, national bestselling author of more than fifty novels, from romance to suspense, loves telling stories.

Born in the US to immigrant parents, Dara enjoys pulling from her Jamaican, British, Nigerian heritage and exposure to various cultures to bring what reviewers and fans call "vivid emotional stories" to life. She is best known for her popular Henson Series, the mysterious Clifton Sisters, and the fun Black Stockings Society.

You can write her at:
contactdara@daragirard.com
or
ILORI Press Books
c/o Dara Girard
P.O. Box 10332
Silver Spring, MD 20914
If you'd like to receive a reply, please send a self-addressed stamped envelope.

Visit her website to sign up for her newsletter and get sneak peeks, monthly updates on new releases, and special offers.